THE EASTER RISING IN SONG & BALLAD

40p

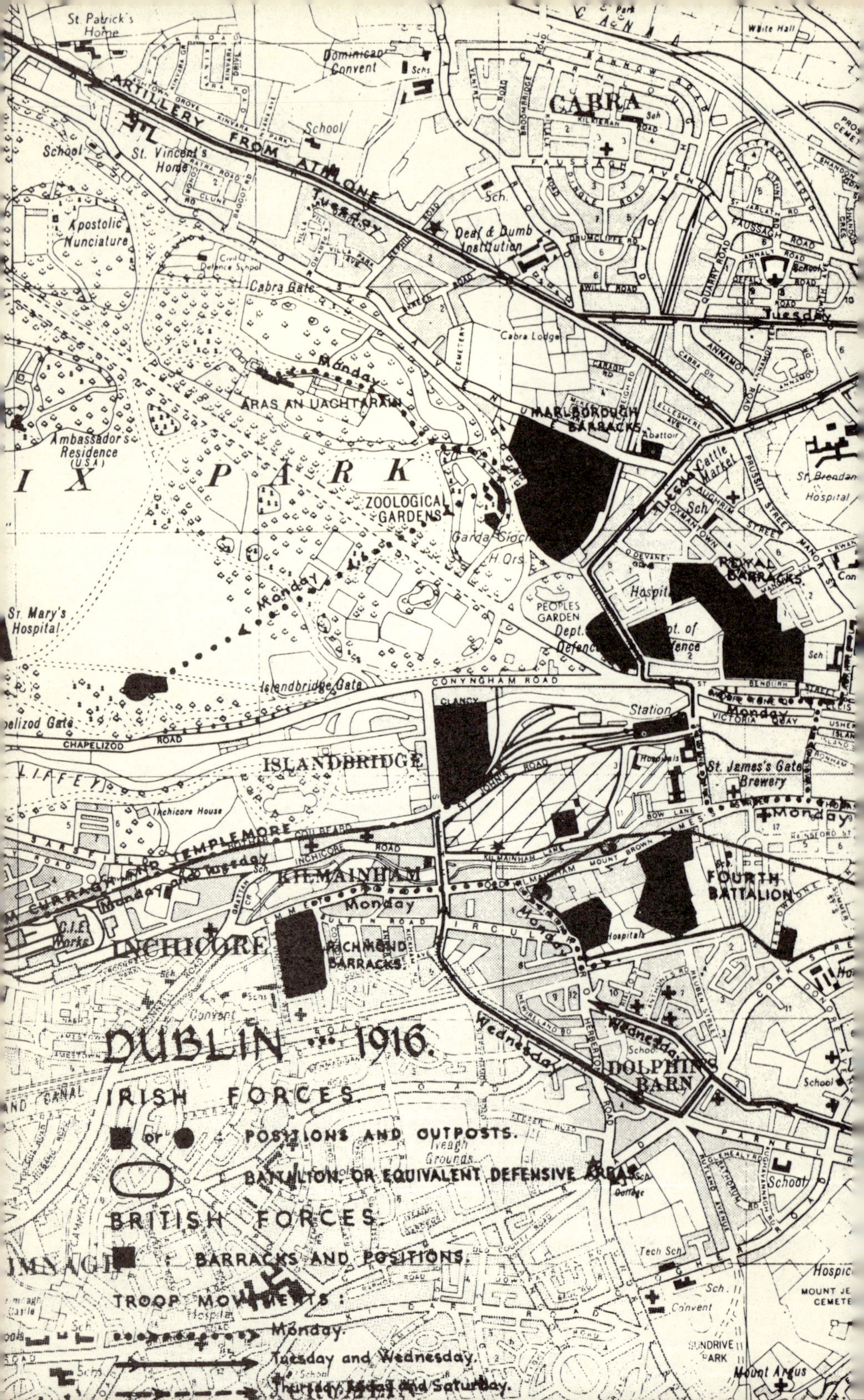

DUBLIN 1916.
IRISH FORCES
■ or ● : POSITIONS AND OUTPOSTS.
BATTALION OR EQUIVALENT DEFENSIVE AREAS
BRITISH FORCES
■ : BARRACKS AND POSITIONS.
TROOP MOVEMENTS :
Monday.
Tuesday and Wednesday.
Thursday Friday and Saturday.
ARTILLERY FROM ATHLONE
Tuesday
Monday
Wednesday
CABRA
St. Patrick's Home
Dominican Convent
St. Vincent's Home
Apostolic Nunciature
Deaf & Dumb Institution
Cabra Gate
Cabra Lodge
ARAS AN UACHTARAIN
Ambassador's Residence (USA)
PARK
ZOOLOGICAL GARDENS
MARLBOROUGH BARRACKS
Abattoir
Cattle Market
St. Brendan's Hospital
ROYAL BARRACKS
PEOPLES GARDEN
St. Mary's Hospital
Islandbridge Gate
CONYNGHAM ROAD
Chapelizod Gate
CHAPELIZOD ROAD
ISLANDBRIDGE
LIFFEY
Station
VICTORIA QUAY
St. James's Gate Brewery
CLANCY
Inchicore House
SARSFIELD ROAD
TEMPLEMORE
CURRAGH
KILMAINHAM
INCHICORE
C.I.E. Works
RICHMOND BARRACKS
FOURTH BATTALION
DOLPHIN'S BARN
CANAL
Convent
School
Tech Sch
Mount Argus
SUNDRIVE PARK

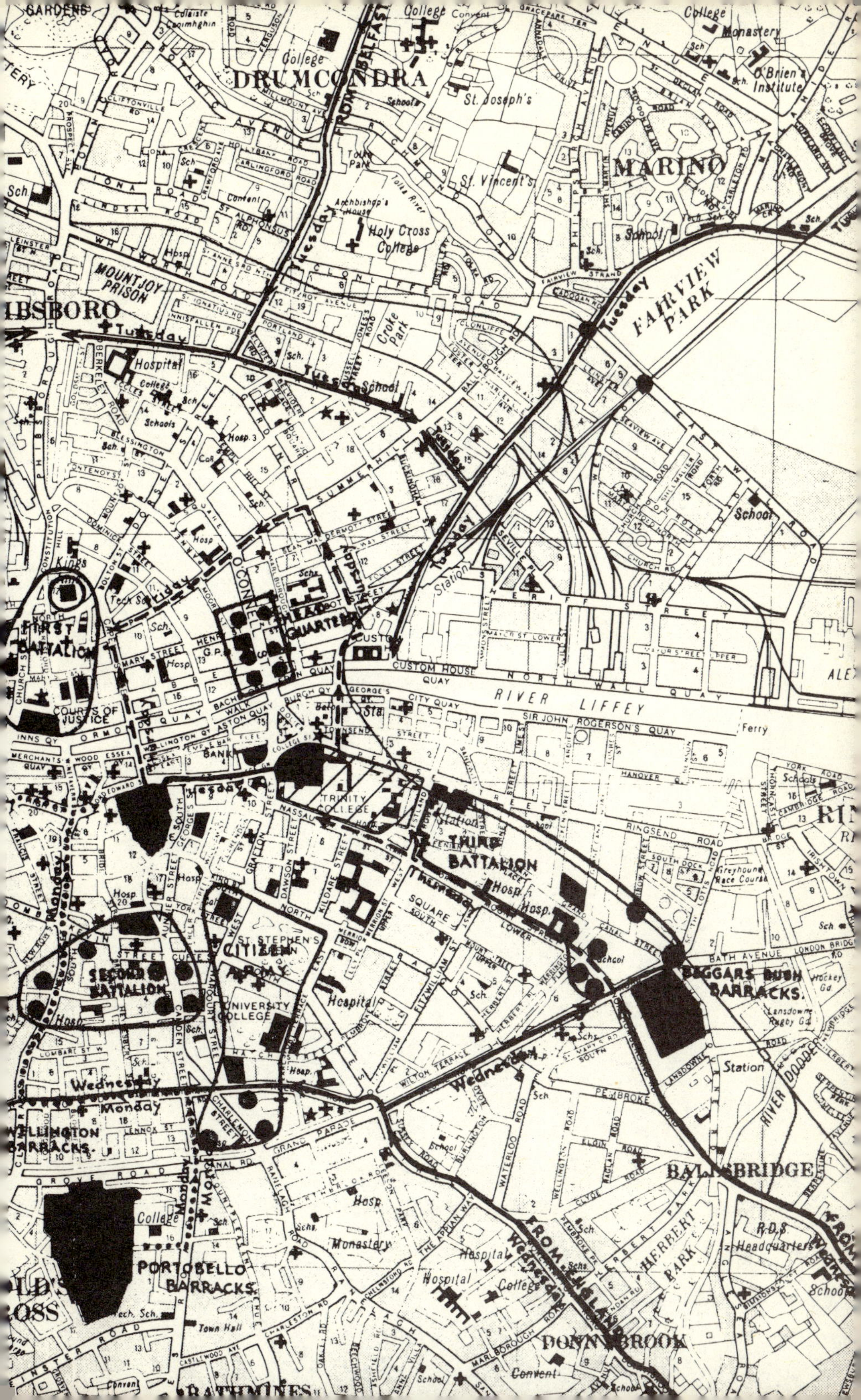

DRUMCONDRA
MARINO
FAIRVIEW PARK
MOUNTJOY PRISON
Croke Park
Holy Cross College
St. Joseph's
St. Vincent's
O'Brien's Institute
FROM BELFAST
Tuesday
FIRST BATTALION
COURTS OF JUSTICE
HEADQUARTERS
RIVER LIFFEY
CUSTOM HOUSE QUAY
NORTH WALL QUAY
SIR JOHN ROGERSON'S QUAY
TRINITY COLLEGE
THIRD BATTALION
Thursday
SECOND BATTALION
CITIZEN ARMY
ST. STEPHEN'S
UNIVERSITY COLLEGE
BEGGARS BUSH BARRACKS.
Wednesday
Monday
WELLINGTON BARRACKS.
PORTOBELLO BARRACKS
BALLSBRIDGE
FROM KINGSTOWN
R.D.S. Headquarters
DONNYBROOK
RATHMINES
RIVER DODDER
Greyhound Race Course
Lansdowne Rugby Gd

THE EASTER RISING IN SONG & BALLAD

C. Desmond Greaves

Kahn & Averill, London
For the Workers' Music Association

First published in 1980 by Stanmore Press Ltd.,
under their associated imprint: Kahn & Averill
for the Workers' Music Association,
236A Westbourne Park Road,
London W11

ISBN 0 900707 51 8 (cloth)
ISBN 0 900707 57 7 (paper)

British Library Cataloguing in Publication Data

The Easter Rising in song & ballad.
1. Folk-songs, Irish - History and criticism
2. Ireland - History - Sinn Feinn Rebellion,
1916 - Songs and music
I. Greaves, Charles Desmond
784.6'8'94150821 ML3654

ISBN 0-900707-51-8
ISBN 0-900707-57-7

Printed in Great Britain by
Lowe & Brydone Printers Limited, Thetford, Norfolk
Bound by J.M. Dent & Sons (Letchworth) Ltd

CONTENTS

Preface 7
Introduction 9
Notating the Harmony 11
1 THE RECORD IN SONG 13
Songs of Our Land 21
A Rebel Song 22
A Soldier's Song 24
The Flag that Floats Above Us 26
The Foggy Dew 27
Who Fears to Speak of Easter Week? 28
2 ORIGINS 30
Down by the Glenside 31
The Magic Flute 32
Whack fol the Diddle 34
The Grand Oul' Dame Britannia 36
The Men of Today 38
Armed for the Battle 40
Ireland Over All 41
Song of Fianna Eireann 42
The Irish Volunteers 44
The Soldiers of Cumann Na mBan 46
My Old Howth Gun 48
The Red Flag 50

3 THE FIGHTING 54
An Dord Feinne 55
Rally Round the Banner Boys 60
The Day 64
Thou Art not Conquered yet Dear Land 66
The West's Asleep 67
Cowld Tay 69
Lonely Banna Strand 72
4 THE AFTERMATH 75
The Dying Soldier 75
The Dead of Easter Week 77
James Connolly the Irish Rebel 79
A Song of Sean MacDermott 81
Bishop O'Dwyer and Maxwell 83
The Three-Coloured Ribbon 86
The Dublin Brigade 87
Slan Libh 88

PREFACE

Some years ago the Workers' Music Association published *Irish Songs of Resistance* which traced in music the story of the Irish struggle against imperialism, from the first invasions. This had a world-wide success and it was felt that another book, this time on the 1916 Rising – which began the modern movement for Irish independence – would be equally well received.

The book which we now publish has been a long time in the making.

Many hands contributed to it; but at a certain stage the WMA felt that it was desirable for one person to be responsible for making a final selection from the material already collected, and if necessary to supplement it and to compose an explanatory text that would give the work the necessary unity of content and form. We were very fortunate that Mr C. Desmond Greaves agreed to undertake this work.

INTRODUCTION

The book is an introduction to a subject which has occupied the attention of many specialists over many years, and some of these are referred to in the appropriate place. There is no new ground broken, and there is nothing definitive about it. It is intended primarily for English readers, but it is hoped that it will not be entirely without value to the Irish.

It has of course been necessary to spell out things which Irish children learn at school. But in view of what they are being urged to forget, perhaps this is no harm. Careful consideration has had to be given to differences between Irish and English musical tradition. In Ireland it was for many years customary to sing unaccompanied. Would it be regarded as a cultural invasion to provide harmony? There are objections in some cases. The intervals of a traditional singer will not necessarily correspond to those of the equally tempered scale, and an attempt to bring them into conformity may restrict the decorations which are the essence of his art. But on the other hand so many people will want accompaniments that, however we might wish to remain purists, we can hardly prohibit others from compromise.

It was felt that if there was to be harmony, it must be professional harmony. Fortunately the WMA has been able to call upon the services of Mr John Jordan, whose long experience of arranging folk music has enabled him to provide harmonizations which should satisfy most critics, and which avoid the pitfalls that lie in the way of those attempting to accompany what may be unfamiliar to them. The system of notation adopted by Mr Jordan is described in a note at the end of this foreword. It consists in essence of the upward figuring of chords from their root. It must be clearly understood that the accompaniments are for those who want them. But it can be justly claimed that those who use them can rely on their sophistication.

The Association's president, Dr Alan Bush has read through the entire work, and while in no way responsible for its deficiencies has made his vast musical learning available at all times. Other members of the Association's committee have been unsparing of their time and patience, and I would like to express appreciation of those who have preferred to remain anonymous. A special word should also be said in appreciation of friends in Dublin who helped with information, transcription and advice, particularly for the translation of the difficult Irish of "An Dord Feinne", which I was then able to put into some kind of English verse.

There were one or two instances where the enquiries that could be completed in the time available failed to reveal the correct or original air for some of the verses, and all I can do is to confess, as others before me, to expeditions of pillage into Davis, Petrie and Bunting.

It would be greatly appreciated if those who can suggest improved versions would be so kind as to draw them to the attention of the WMA, so that they can be considered for use in the future.

Finally I would like to express appreciation of Messrs Waltons of North Frederick Street for permission to reproduce material subject to their copyright; also to Mrs Eileen O'Casey for permission to reprint her late husband's "Grand Oul' Dame Britannia", and to the Controller, Stationery Office, Dublin, and the Military History Society of Ireland, for permission to reproduce the map on p. 57.

C.D.G.

NOTATING THE HARMONY

The scales used in folk songs vary considerably. Some contain only five notes, others six or seven; that is to say they can be pentatonic, hexatonic or heptatonic like the modern major or minor scales. All of these scales take various modal forms, and the matter is not exhausted even then. In this book an effort has been made to provide an arrangement which suits the special style of each air.

The accompanying instruments will of course be provided at least with the seven notes of the modern scale. But they may not necessarily all be used. Some notes will not be sounded. Some chords, in airs based on six or five-note scales, when viewed from the standpoint of the heptatonic scale, will lack a third, fifth or seventh. In order to facilitate the accompanist a system of numbering has been used, based on a seven-note scale.

Figured bass is only of use when the bass note is written. Therefore another method has been adopted. The bass note could of course have been indicated, but the setting out of a complete bass line for all these songs would have doubled the cost of copying and printing. Instead, the name of the note required to determine the accompaniment has been written *above* the treble clef. But this note will only signify the actual bass when the chord denoted is in root position. Thus if C is the root, and the seven notes above are numbered according to their intervals (D2, E3, F4, G5, A6, Bb or

B7), a first inversion of the tonic chord upon C will be indicated by C (3, 5, 1). The bass note in this case will of course be E, though C is written above the clef. It is the first *figure* which indicates the actual bass note, not the letter. The 5-1, could of course be played as 1-5 without changing the character of the chord. It is the bass note that is sacrosanct.

In the case of the higher discords the dominant eleventh in the key of C would be written G^{11} (135724), the index attached to the letter G indicating the maximum interval from the root. But 2 and 4 are written instead of 9 and 11. These chords are not frequently played in full. It is probably best to omit 3, but to keep the greater intervals to the upper part of the chord, for example to play 15724, 15742 or 15247 according to fingering and taste.

The use of the letter 'm' over the treble note indicates that the accompanying chord is derived from the minor scale.

In the case of chords derived from the five and six-note scales, notes that would be sounded in chords derived from heptatonic scales may be missing. Consequently C^7 might be indicated C^7 (137) or C^7 (157) because the G or the E was not present in the scale.

For stylistic reasons the performer desiring to use harmony is recommended to play only the notes indicated by the figures where they occur. Doubling is of course allowed.

J.J.

1

THE RECORD IN SONG

> Starting thus, Ireland may yet set the torch to a European Conflagration that will not burn out until the last throne and the last capitalist bond and debenture, will be shrivelled on the pyre of the last war lord. — James Connolly

The insurrection of Easter 1916 was the most spectacular event of the Irish revolution. With less than a thousand men, the rebels seized key points in Dublin and held them for a week against forces immeasurably superior in numbers and equipment. They ran up the green, white and orange tricolour on the roof of the General Post Office in O'Connell Street, which became their headquarters. They proclaimed an independent Irish republic and decreed civil and religious liberty, equal rights and equal opportunities for all citizens. There were lesser irruptions in the provinces, notably in the south of Co. Galway.

The Rising burst like a thunderclap on the deliberations of a Cabinet at last, after two years of war, seriously concerned over England's prospects. Uneasy men weighed distasteful alternatives. A negotiated peace, or a pyrrhic victory? Social strains were appearing in Britain. Already in Scotland working class militants were in jail. The revolt in Ireland bore directly on the issue of peace. The defeated side could expect to lose colonies, the victors to gain them. The cry went up, "The Germans are behind this." Fear whetted the appetite for vengeance, and after the rebels were bloodily defeated there began the sordid train of court martial, execution, imprisonment and deportation.

As often happens tyranny over-reached itself. As a whole the Irish people had not been in a revolutionary mood. They were enjoying the first brief prosperity in living memory. They did not wish this to be disturbed. Again, many Irishmen were fighting for England, and their dependents were in receipt of Government allowances.

Agriculture was flourishing and there was work in the towns. So some of the Dublin crowds hissed the insurgent prisoners as they were led away. They were against them for the Rising. But soon they were for them for the executions. Fifteen men were shot, and the sixteenth, Casement, was hanged. All this conformed to a pattern the people recognised. Connolly and Pearse took their places beside Tone and Emmet in the great national martyrology of Ireland.

The rebels went out to establish an independent republic. But the beneficiaries of their sacrifice were the moderate Sinn Fein party which as such took no part in the Rising. But before it swept the country in the General Election of December 1918, a mass movement had arisen which breathed a new fire into it. At the back of this movement were the organised workers, their trade unions vastly strengthened in number and bargaining power, at a time when their rulers were utterly dependent on them if the war was to be won. Four-fifths of the electorate voted for separation from England. Here was a clear mandate. The Sinn Fein Members of Parliament declined to take their seats at Westminster. They established a revolutionary assembly, Dail Eireann, which met in Dublin on 21st January 1919 and issued a declaration of independence and a domestic programme.

But London did not recognize the right of the Irish people to national self-determination. The English Government claimed that the unit of sovereignty was the United Kingdom. From the conflict of rights arose a dual power. For two and a half years police, soldiers and "black and tans" strove to terrify the Irish people from their allegiance to Dail Eireann.

The result was a constantly intensifying guerrilla war.

What of the minority who did not want an independent republic? These, comprising only a fifth of the population, resided for the most part in the extreme north-east of the country. They had long been marked out as the recipients of special favours. Industrial development, municipal amenity, favourable price differentials all contributed towards the "loyalty" of the north-east. They were not consulted about their future. But they learned to accept it. The Unionists, so called from wishing to continue the Union of 1801, were detached from the rest of Ireland, and a separate administration was established in which they were a majority. A further tenth of the population of Ireland was added to them. These people belonged to the majority of the Irish people but were made into a minority within a minority. The leaders of the majority then fell out among themselves over the acceptance or rejection of this arrangement, and a bloody civil war ensued in which the Republic of 1919 was extinguished and replaced by Dominion status.

Thus the revolution was crushed. A veil was then drawn over the past. It has been observed that nothing is consigned to so deep an oblivion as the motives of an unsuccessful revolution. Little indeed was recalled of the partially successful one. And that little was slanted to the advantage of the new incumbents of office. The world was told that the Irish problem was solved. The Irish had got what they wanted. They could not agree so they separated. The truncated twenty-six-county state was passed off as the Republic, its shortcomings being used to discredit republicanism. The democratic purposes of the Rising, the principles of the revolutionary leaders, went into obscurity.

But the songs of the revolution told another story. Frequently sentimental, at times wildly romantic, of literary and musical quality as varied as the talents and circumstances of those who wrote them, Irish songs gave a truer folk history than the card-indexes of the colleges, because they recorded the emotions of the common people, emotions recalled often enough when the events that occasioned them might be partly forgotten.

Such was the position until the nineteen-sixties when a series of important centenaries and jubilees acquainted the young people with their nation's forgotten past. James Connolly in particular was not only rediscovered but became the special hero of the new generation.

Most of the songs here assembled fall into the general category of "street ballads". As G.D. Zimmermann observes in his important book* their origins are heterogeneous. In England today the political ballad is extinct. The commercial popular song, while musically more sophisticated, confines itself to sentiments likely to be widely acceptable among those who buy its recordings. Party songs are unknown. Nobody wishes to hang the Prime Minister "on a sour apple tree." Yet at the end of the last century scarcely any important political event escaped the sympathy or satire of rhymesters who could furnish words in a trice to any well-known tune, which would usually be drawn from the music hall, and in turn fertilize that institution by retroaction.

In Ireland music-hall ditties jostled with traditional airs of immense antiquity, and the genus is not yet extinct though more sparsely distributed. The style of the street songs was of course the product of long tradition. The words were often murdered, but according to a well-understood ritual. Elements were derived from Gaelic poetry, for example assonant and internal rhyme, as well as from Irish harp music in much of which there is a strong modal legacy.

Mr Sean O'Boyle in his valuable *Irish Song Tradition*† stresses that "a proper appreciation of Irish music is impossible without a knowledge of the language." This is not difficult to understand. Everybody can detect the trochaic tendency of German and appreciate its influence on the classical *Lied.* The word order and therefore the inherent stress of the Irish sentence is quite different, and the general rhythm tends to be anapaestic. This and the tradition of internal rhyme have their influence on musical phrasing. Some of

**Songs of Irish rebellion 1780-1900*, (Dublin, Allen Figgis, 1967; Folklore Music Associates, U.S.A. 1967)

†Gilbert Dalton, Dublin 1976.

the features of Irish music derive from traditions of extreme antiquity, and express in microcosm at least a thousand years of Irish history. Since Irish history is not taught in British schools, it may be useful to say something about how this happens.

The Romans never conquered Ireland. As a result there survived for close on fifteen hundred years a system of society which did not recognize private property in land, which preserved gentile institutions once distributed throughout Europe, and developed them to an extent that was found nowhere else. That ancient forms were preserved does not mean that they remained "primitive", and as late as the time of James I of England and VI of Scotland, Francis Bacon described Ireland as:

> endowed with so many dowries of nature (considering the fruitfulness of the soil, the ports, the rivers, the fishings, the quarries, the woods and other materials, and especially the race and generation of men, valiant, hard and active) as it is not easy, no not upon the continent, to find such confluence of commodities.

This was the picture of a wealthy and prosperous society, one which could and did maintain a substantial leisured class. There was a highly developed system of law. There were great educational institutions, sophisticated poetry in which satire played an important part, and a substantial "art music". Giraldus Cambrensis recorded his opinion that the Irish harpers were the most accomplished musicians in the world, and indeed when it is remembered that they served a twelve-year apprenticeship, this becomes credible.

All this was finally smashed in the seventeenth century. As Spenser had put it, the Irishman was to be brought "so low that he shall have no heart or ability to endure his wretchedness . . . so pluck him on his knees that he will never be able to stand again."

The last of the native aristrocracy had been driven abroad by 1691. Cromwell had driven the native occupants of the land across the Shannon. Those found to the east of it became helots. Thousands of girls were sold as slaves to the

Barbados. Though his regime could not be maintained in its full fury, the poets became beggars; the educators became hedge-schoolmasters; the harpers became highly respected but impoverished itinerants. So complete was the devastation that official historians, glad to have the telling of such a story, could deny the very existence of an Irish culture which the rulers of England had destroyed. What followed was a massive intermingling of aristocratic and plebeian elements, in which of course the latter constantly increased in importance.

It is however of interest to try to glimpse this culture from its earlier stages to the period of its greatest development. Unfortunately this can scarcely be done with certainty. It has been pointed out that while everybody knows of the importance of harp music in Ireland before the conquest, nobody knows what it sounded like. It was not until the first decades of the nineteenth century that Edward Bunting, formerly organist at Armagh, undertook his life's work of collecting what harp music survived. The tradition had been considerably modified and the harp itself had fallen into disuse.

Musicologists have tried to deduce the past from the present. Early this century Grattan Flood claimed to have carefully examined several thousand Irish airs (incidentally proving the Irish origin of many so-called Scottish airs) and drawn the conclusion that they were largely pentatonic in origin. He went further and suggested that it was possible to trace a distinct Gaelic modal system based on a pentachord, providing five modes when each note in turn served as tonic or final. There were thus no semitones, and motion of a tone and a half was not regarded as a leap.*

Anybody familiar with Irish traditional singing will recognise the pentatonic element. This is of course not to suggest that the Irish have a monopoly of pentatonism. Indeed it would be natural from the theory of sound to expect that

*I would like to call this interval a sesquitone so as to conceal in Latin the duality of a tone and a half tone. But of course it is only constant in the equally tempered chromatic scale, where it is derived from the octave, or first harmonic.

the fourth and seventh degrees of the major scale should appear last, the latter representing a very remote harmonic of the fundamental, the former requiring an act of imagination, shifting the fundamental to a note of one-third its frequency – an act we all perform today without the slightest difficulty.

It is useful when singing Irish songs to remember this pentatonic legacy, though it should not be obtruded or made too much of. The famous "Danny Boy" is in the Ionian mode, but it is an interesting experiment to play it without sounding the fourth or seventh degrees, for example in place of the first leading note to play the dominant. It is surprising how much of it will be found to survive the treatment. At the same time it will be clear how inevitable it was that the pentatonic scale should evolve into the heptatonic.

This has, of course, been known for centuries in Ireland. And Mr Sean O'Boyle offers evidence from the stringing of Irish harps of a period when the intermediate hexatonic scale held the field. It was not that the modern scale developed late in Ireland, but that its predecessor was exceptionally developed. It must be remembered that there were several centuries after the fall of Rome when Ireland was the intellectual centre of north-western Europe. And with this in mind people have sometimes suggested that here is one of those historical vistas down which we can glimpse a small part of the character of the world Rome itself destroyed.

The sickly harmonizations of Irish airs that have become universally popular arise very frequently from ignorance or neglect of the modal substratum. As a general rule no note should be used in the harmony that is not present in the melody.

Bunting in his *Ancient Music of Ireland* divided all Irish music into heptatonic and non-heptatonic, but spoke of each category's giving special prominence to the (Ionian) sub-mediant. Perhaps this indicates that the seventh was once absent, so that motion to the tonic would not be felt as a leap. Writers have referred to the Irish "gapped scale" but this is to stand historical development on its head.

Mr Sean O'Boyle has noted how Bunting tried to understand traditional Irish music in terms of the classical style, which is of course impossible. Yet how well such modern writers as Percy French have held to the ancient principles, and thereby pleased their hearers, may be illustrated from "Phil the Fluter's Ball", where the fourth is not once sounded, and the seventh never receives the down beat.

The air of "The Foggy Dew" (obtained by Bunting from James McKnight, a native Irish speaker from the Co. Down) could well derive from a pentatonic A mode. There are other characteristics of Irish music which have been dealt with by Mr O'Boyle and others. The native Irish is only one element of the music we are discussing, but it is the element we neglect at our peril. It must be treated with the greatest respect.

Of ancient Irish civilization perhaps it may therefore be said that its music survived better than its edifices. At the beginning of the nineteenth century individual enthusiasts like Bunting were travelling the country recording the music of the harpers, and for many years Comhaltas Ceoltoiri has preserved a tradition of living performance and draws thousands to the annual Feis Ceol. Just as bards, jurists and noblemen became fugitives and beggars, fusing with the popular mass from which they had been differentiated, so Irish music presents a recombination of plebeian and aristocratic traditions sharing a common national character.

The deliberate use of song for political purposes is well attested. Liliburlero whistled *Seamus a' chacha** out of three kingdoms. The United Irishmen had broadsheets. In the forties Thomas Davis designed to teach through song the Irish history the English ascendancy were suppressing. Jim Connell, John Leslie and James Connolly attempted the same for the Labour movement. Everybody has heard of Connell's "Red Flag" and many know Connolly's "Rebel Song", though Connolly was not outstandingly successful as a ballad writer.

*James II.

SONGS OF OUR LAND

The bards may go down to the place of their slumbers;
The lyre of the charmer be hushed in the grave;
But far in the future the power of their numbers
Shall kindle the hearts of our faithful and brave.
It will waken an echo in souls deep and lonely,
Like voices of reeds by the summer breeze fanned;
It will call up a spirit of freedom when only
Her breathings are heard in the songs of our land.

For they keep a record of those the true-hearted,
Who fell with the cause they had vowed to maintain,
They show us bright shadows of glories departed,
Of the love that grew cold and the hope that was vain.
The page may be lost and the pen long forsaken,
And weeds may grow wild o'er the brave heart and hand;
But ye are still left when all else has been taken,
Like streams in the desert, sweet songs of our land.

Songs of our land! ye have followed the stranger
With power over ocean and desert afar;
Ye have gone with our wand'rers thro' distance and danger;
And gladdened their path like a home-guiding star;
With the breath of our mountains in summers long vanished
And visions that passed like a wave from our strand;
With hope for their country and joy from her banished,
Ye come to us ever, sweet songs of our land.

The springtime may come with the song of her glory,
To bid the green heart of the forest rejoice;
But the pine of the mountain tho' blasted and hoary
And rock in the desert can send forth a voice.
It is thus in their triumphs for deep desolations,
While ocean waves roll, or the mountains shall stand,
Still hearts that are bravest and best of the nations,
Shall glory and live in the songs of our land.

Frances Browne

A REBEL SONG

We sing no more of wailing,
And no songs of sighs or tears,
High are our hopes and stout our hearts,
And banished all our fears.
Our flag is raised above us,
So that all the world may see,
'Tis Labour's faith and Labour's arm
Alone can Labour free.

Chorus

Out of the depths of misery,
We march with hearts aflame,
With wrath against the rulers false,
Who wreck our manhood's name.
The serf who licks the tyrant's rod,
May bend forgiving knee;
The slave who breaks his slav'ry's chain,
A wrathful man must be.

Chorus

Our army marches onward,
With its face towards the dawn,
In trust secure in that one thing,
The slave may lean upon.
The might within the arm of him,
Who knowing freedom's worth,
Strikes hard to banish tyranny,
From off the face of earth.

Chorus

James Connolly

In his famous poem on Easter week W.B. Yeats was tempted to wonder whether his writings had helped to inspire any of its participants to take part in it. The suggestion is not far-fetched. One of the currents of ideas influencing the desire for Irish independence was that of the literary revival sparked off by Standish O'Grady and expressing itself further in the work of Lady Gregory. Pearse, MacDonagh and Casement were serious minor poets. Among the song and ballad writers was Peadar Kearney, author of the national anthem. Sean O'Casey did not take part in the rising, but can be credited with helping to prepare the political scene. Sean Connolly was an actor and singer. And James Connolly as well as his well-known Labour songs, has to his credit the patriotic play *Under Which Flag,* which was performed at Liberty Hall shortly before the Rising. There is obviously a profound significance in a movement which can unite within its ambit the most advanced representatives of the working class and the cream of the national intelligentsia.

A SOLDIER'S SONG

In valley green, on towering crag, our fathers fought before us,
And conquered 'neath the same old flag that's proudly floating o'er us;

> We're children of a fighting race,
> That never yet has known disgrace,
> And as we march, the foe to face,
> We'll chant a soldier's song.

Sons of the Gael, men of the Pale, the long watched day is breaking,
The serried ranks of Innisfail shall set the tyrant quaking;

> Our camp fires now are burning low,
> See in the east the silvery glow,
> Out yonder waits the Saxon foe,
> Then chant a soldier's song.

Peadar Kearney

The prominence of poets and players has a twofold significance. First, the Rising was the work of the "petite bourgeoisie and a part of the working class." Second, the revolution of which it formed a part had as its object national liberation, and one of the purposes for which separation from England was desired was the defence, revival and development of Irish culture. There was also a deep sense of history. Though the most strategically placed and defensible building in Dublin may have been thought to be the Bank of Ireland, it is said that Pearse refused to have it put at risk. It had been the old Parliament House before the Union of 1801. The green, white and orange tricolour adopted as the flag of the Republic was derived from an orange, white and green predecessor, woven by the women of the municipality of Paris and presented to Thomas Francis Meagher who visited the city in 1848. It symbolised the unity of Protestant and Catholic through the attainment of liberty, equality and fraternity.

The sense of history, giving universal significance to the events of the day, pervades most of "The Foggy Dew". The war between English and German imperialism had been expected for years and was the subject of a voluminous literature. Without the consent of the full Cabinet, Asquith and two of his ministers had given secret assurances to Poincaré that England would assist France in the event of a conflict with Germany. On the outbreak of war the full Cabinet at first declined to recommend Parliament to honour these pledges. A second Cabinet meeting was called, and it was then, according to Scawen Blunt, that Asquith trotted out the neutrality of Belgium. Under the slogan of "the freedom of small nations" English soldiers were deployed in five continents. The reference to Wild Geese is to the emigration of the Irish armed forces after the surrender of Limerick in 1691. The Irishmen participating in the war were being forced out of their homeland by deliberately created unemployment.

THE FLAG THAT FLOATS ABOVE US

No hireling servile slaves are we,
To bend with meek submission
To the alien's grinding tyranny,
Or despot's fierce ambition;
But for our own, our suffering land,
Our foreign foes defying,
We'll strike while we can raise a hand
And keep that banner flying.

A living rampart round it throng,
A thousand hands are ready
To strike a blow for motherland,
Calm, patient, firm and steady!
Then shout it out to foe and friend,
To those who hate or love us,
While life remains we will defend
The flag that floats above us.

William Collins

THE FOGGY DEW

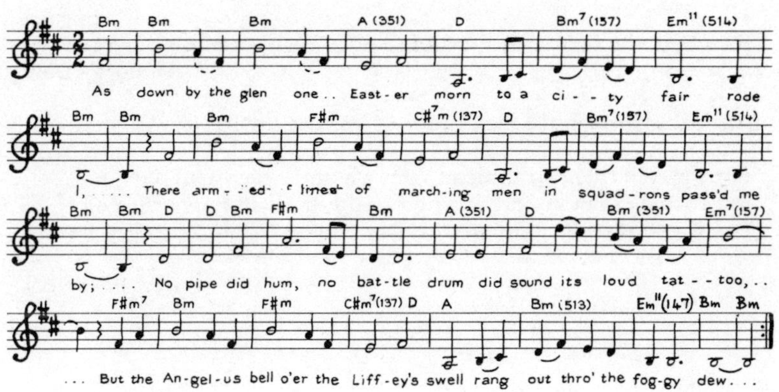

Right proudly high in Dublin Town they flung out the flag of war,
'Twas better to die 'neath an Irish sky than at Suvla or Sud El Bar;
And from the plains of Royal Meath strong men came hurrying through
While Britannia's Huns, with their great big guns, sailed in through the Foggy Dew.

O' the night fell back, and the rifle's crack made "Perfidious Albion" reel
'Mid the leaden rain seven tongues of flame did shine o'er the lines of steel;
By each shining blade a prayer was said that to Ireland her sons be true
And when morning broke still the war flag shook out its folds in the Foggy Dew.

'Twas England bade our Wild Geese go that small nations might be free,
But their lonely graves are by Suvla's waves or the fringe of the great North Sea.
O, had they died by Pearse's side, or had fought with Cathal Brugha,
Their names we'd keep where the Fenians sleep, 'neath the shroud of the Foggy Dew.

But the bravest fell, and the requiem bell rang mournfully and clear,
For those who died that Eastertide in the springtime of the year;
While the world did gaze, with deep amaze, at those fearless men, but few
Who bore the fight that Freedom's light might shine through the Foggy Dew.

Ah! back through the glen I rode again, and my heart with grief was sore
For I parted then with valiant men whom I never shall see more;
But to and fro in my dreams I go, and I kneel and pray for you,
For slavery fled, O glorious dead! when you fell in the Foggy Dew.

Rev. P. O'Neill

The song "Who Fears to Speak of Easter Week?" is an adaptation of "Who Fears to Speak of Ninety-eight?" which was written in one night by John Kells Ingram when he was a student at Trinity College in the days of "Young Ireland."

WHO FEARS TO SPEAK OF EASTER WEEK?

The spirit wave that came to save
  The peerless Celtic soul,
From earthly strain of greed to gain
  Had caught them in its roll;
Had swept them high to do or die,
  To sound a trumpet call:
For true men though few men
  To follow one and all.

Upon their shield a stainless field,
  With virtues blazoned bright;
With Temperance and Purity
  And Truth and Honour right.
So now they stand at God's Right Hand,
  Who famed their dauntless clay,
Who taught them and brought them
  The glory of to-day.

The storied page of this our age
  Will save our land from shame.
The ancient foe had boasted – ho!
  That Irishmen were tame.
  They bought their souls for paltry doles,
  And told the world of slaves,
That lie, men! shall die, men!
  In Pearse and Plunkett's graves.

The brave who've gone to linger on
  Beneath the tyrant's heel –
We know they pray another day
  With clash of clanging steel.
Now from their cell their voices swell,
  And loudly call to you.
Then ask men! the task, men!
  That yet remains to do.

2

ORIGINS

Among the organizations concerned with the preparation of the Rising, pride of place must be given to the I.R.B., the Irish Republican Brotherhood. P.S. O'Hegarty* emphasized its all-embracing national interest in words that may sound exaggerated.

> Strange and transient Committees and Societies were constantly cropping up, doing this and that specific national work. The I.R.B. formed them. The I.R.B. ran them. The I.R.B. provided the money. The I.R.B. dissolved them when their work was done.

The Fenians, as the early members of the I.R.B. were called, were established in 1858, by men who had taken part in the abortive revolts of 1848 and 1849. Within a few years they established a mass organization throughout Ireland and penetrated the British Army. Their aim was an independent republic. Their chosen means was armed insurrection. But without a continental revolution or an external war diverting England's energies, what could be the prospect of success? The Rising of 1867 was undertaken without waiting for these preconditions of victory. After its failure the prisons were crammed with patriots and a considerable ballad literature was prompted by the ensuing amnesty movement. Following the defeat of the open insurrection, one section of the movement turned to Blanquist "Propaganda by the Deed",

* *The Victory of Sinn Fein* (Talbot Press, Dublin 1922)

and the gun-barrels and powder kegs came into their own. Other sections worked with Parnell and Davitt in the open mass agitations of the Land League and Home Rule Movement. There was some cross-fertilization between the two sections, and indeed while the tradition of the Land League greatly influenced Connolly, Tom Clarke derived from the Blanquist section.

Peadar Kearney's "Down by the Glenside" recalls the traditional *Aisling* in which the narrator meets a female figure, in this case an old women, who personifies Ireland and raises the demand for freedom.

DOWN BY THE GLENSIDE

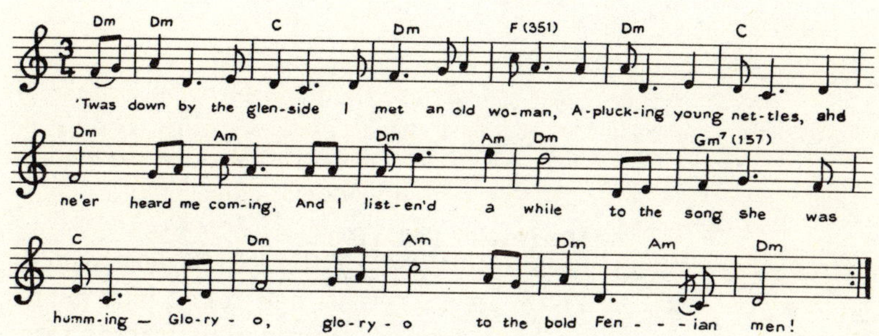

'Tis fifty long years since I saw the moon beaming
On strong manly forms and on eyes with hope gleaming,
I see them again, sure, through all my day-dreaming,
Glory-o, glory-o to the bold Fenian men!

Some died by the wayside, some died 'mid the stranger,
And wise men have told us, their cause was a failure,
But they stood by old Ireland, and they never feared danger,
Glory-o, glory-o to the bold Fenian men!

I passed on my way, God be praised that I met her,
Be life long or short, I will never forget her,
We may have been brave men, but we'll never have better,
Glory-o, glory-o to the bold Fenian men!

Peadar Kearney

When under the influence of the gathering storm the I.R.B. began to revive, after some internal turmoil, a group of talented young men appeared on the scene, and, with the encouragement of the veteran Fenian Tom Clarke, issued a remarkable monthly called *Irish Freedom*. Like Davis's *Nation* and Nielson's *Northern Star*, this was one of the great periodicals of Irish history. It published "A Soldier's Song" in 1912, and encouraged its writers in a form of witty satire of which "The Magic Flute" is probably the best example. This so deliciously takes off the bullet-headed implacability of a certain type of sectarian Protestant, that people have sometimes imagined it to be an Orange song.

THE MAGIC FLUTE

But the treacherous scoundrel he took us all in,
For he married a Papish called Bridget McGinn;
Turned Papish himself, and forsook the old cause
That gave us our freedom, religion, and laws.
Now, the boys in the townland made some noise upon it,
And Bob had to fly to the province of Connacht.
He flew with his wife and fixings to boot,
And along with the others the ould Orange flute.

At Chapel on Sundays to atone for past deeds,
He'd say Pater and Aves, and counted his beads,
Till, after some time, at the priest's own desire,
He went with that old flute to play in the choir.
He went with the ould flute to play in the loft,
But the instrument shivered and sighed and then coughed
When he blew it and fingered it, it made a strange noise,
For the flute would play only "The Protestant Boys".

Bob jumped up and started and got in a flutter,
And he put the ould flute in the bless'd holy water;
He thought that it might now make some other sound,
When he blew it again it played "Croppies, Lie Down!"
And all he did whistle, and finger, and blow,
To play Papish music he found it "no go."
"Kick the Pope," "The Boyne Water," and such like 'twould sound,
But one Papish squeak in it couldn't be found.

At a council of priests that was held the next day,
They decided to banish the ould flute away;
As they couldn't knock heresy out its head,
They bought Bob another to play in its stead.
So the ould flute was doomed and its fate was pathetic,
It was fastened and burned at the stake as heretic.
While the flames roared around it, they heared a strange noise,
'Twas the ould flute still whistlin' "The Protestant Boys"

Nugent Bohem

And if the Orangeman must take his medicine in this, the condescending paternalism of Westminster which would do anything for Ireland except get out of it, is satirized in Kearney's "Whack fol the Diddle."

WHACK FOL THE DIDDLE

When we were savage, fierce and wild,
Whack fol the diddle lol the di do day,
She came as a mother to her child,
Whack fol the didle lol the di do day,
Gently raised us from the slime,
Kept our hands from hellish crime,
And sent us to heaven in her own good time,
Whack fol the diddle lol the di do day.

Our fathers oft' were naughty boys,
Whack fol the diddle lol the di do day,
Pikes and guns are dangerous toys,
Whack fol the diddle lol the di do day.
From Beal an Atha Buidhe to Pleter's Hill
They made poor England weep her fill,
But old Britannia loves us still,
Whack fol the diddle lol the di do day.

Oh Irishmen forget the past,
Whack fol the diddle lol the di do day,
And think of the day that is coming fast,
Whack fol the diddle lol the di do day.
When we shall all be civilised,
Neat and clean and well advised,
Oh won't Mother England be surprised!
Whack fol the diddle lol the di do day.

Chorus.

Whack fol the diddle lol the di do day,
So we say Hip Hurrah!
Come and listen while we pray,
Whack fol the diddle lol the di do day.

Peadar Kearney

The satirical tradition, which is of immense antiquity in Irish literature was continued by Sean O'Casey whose "Grand Oul' Dame Britannia" was published in James Connolly's *Workers' Republic.* John Redmond, referred to in the song, was the leader of the Irish Parliamentary Party which had pledged Irish men and resources to the English war effort.

THE GRAND OUL' DAME BRITANNIA

Och! Ireland, sure I'm proud of you—
        Ses the Grand Oul' Dame Britannia,
To poor little Belgium tried and true,
        Ses the Grand Oul' Dame Britannia.
Ye've closed your ear to the Sinn Fein lies,
For you know each Gael that for England dies
Will enjoy Home Rule in the clear blue skies,
        Ses the Grand Oul' Dame Britannia.

Oh, Casement! Damn that Irish pig, (ses....)*
Wee'll make him dance an English jig.
But Redmond's here – the good and great,
A pillar of the English State.
Who fears to speak of '98?

The Castle's now an altered place,
It's the Drawing Room of the Irish race.
John Redmond to the throne is bowed
'Mid a frantic cheering Irish crowd.
Sure it's like the days of Shane the Proud.

*After the first, second and last line of each verse, repeat "ses the Grand Oul' Dame Britannia".

For Redmond now Home Rule has won,
And he's finished what Wolfe Tone begun.
Yet rebels through the country stalk,
Shouting '67 and "Bachelors Walk";*
Did ye ever hear such foolish talk?

Ye want a pound or two from me!
For your oul' Hibernian Academy!
Don't you know we've got the Huns to quell,
And we want the cash for shot and shell.
Your artists! – Let them go to hell.

Ah Scholars, Hurlers, Saints and Bards!
Come along an' list in the Irish Guards,
Each man that treads on a German's foot
'Ill be given a parcel tied up neat –
Of a Tombstone Cross and a winding sheet..

Be jabers, Redmond, you're the Bhoy!
Sure you're Ireland's pride and England's joy.
Like a true born Gael he faced the Hun,
Then he jumped around an' he fired a gun.
Faix, you should have seen the Germans run!

Sure I spoke today with Inspector Quinn,
An' he told me straight we were bound to win!
What mean these deafening newsboys' yells?
What tale is this the paper tells?
A British retreat from the Dardanelles.

Sean O'Casey

***Refers to the shooting of an unarmed crowd on Bachelor's Walk by the side of the Liffey after the Howth gun-running in August 1914.**

There is a healthy rugged optimism in the songs of *Irish Freedom* and the *Workers' Republic.* The latter was founded in May 1915 after *Irish Freedom* and the *Irish Worker* had been suppressed by the authorities. It was printed under armed guard at Liberty Hall. This was a movement which intended to fight and win. But the old-style laments for lost causes continued to be popular, perhaps too popular, some of the revolutionaries believed.

THE MEN OF TODAY

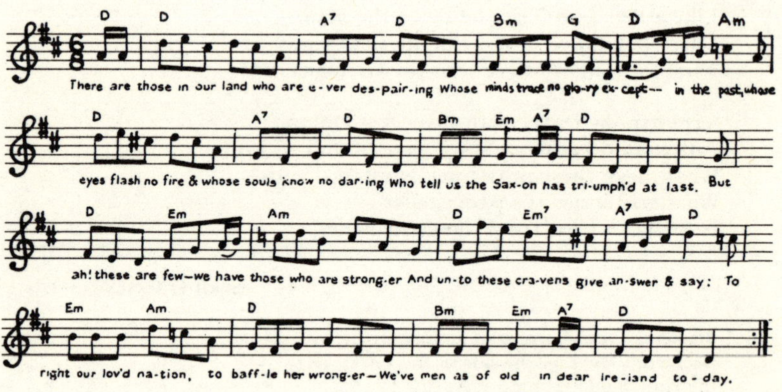

They would have us believe that men stalwart as Brian,
As brave as those soldiers who drove out the Dane,
As bold as Red Hugh, who had heart like a lion,
Shall never be seen in our island again;
They say that the valour of Conn has departed,
That prostrate and weak in the dust we must stay;
But our answer is – No! for men staunch and stouthearted
As ever have lived are in Ireland today.

These creatures despondent deny we inherit
The strong iron nerve of Fitzgerald and Tone,
And Emmet's pure manhood and Grattan's proud spirit
They say from our country forever have flown.
They libel their kinsmen while thus they are whining;
For us, we believe, let them shrink as they may,
That courage lives on and that virtue is shining
As brightly as ever in Ireland today

Yes, men with the strength and the faith of past ages
Are here with us now, marching towards the same end;
We've scholars and statesmen and soldiers and sages,
With spirits no tyrants can conquer or bend;
And ever, till Ireland has worsted the spoilers,
Till falls on her white brow blest Liberty's rays,
Her cause will be championed by hosts of such toilers,
As those who beat onward her banner today.

Daniel Crilly

Before "A Soldier's Song" won acceptance, there was a search for a worthy national anthem. "God Save Ireland, said the Heroes" to the tune of "Tramp, Tramp, Tramp, the Boys are Marching," suffered from a number of objections, and was felt to be linked with the Parliamentarians. A story is told of Parnell asking the band in a restaurant to play "Tramp, Tramp, Tramp" and causing astonishment when his entire party stood up. The Americans had "John Brown" and Countess Markiewicz set words to a Polish hymn and produced the "Battle Hymn of the Irish Republic", which begins well though its author lacked the technique to sustain it.

ARMED FOR THE BATTLE

The spirit of freedom floats on the ether,
Souls of our heroes march by our side.
Tone is our battle cry: Emmet inspires us,
Those who for freedom fall never shall die,
England is breaking: shout we exultant;
England is beaten! Ireland is free!
Charge for the old cause: down with the old foe!
Giving our heart's blood Ireland to free!

Constance Markiewicz

When Joseph Haydn was in London he was impressed by the custom of singing "God Save the King" on all public occasions. He believed it had been the means of strengthening the national coherence of the English people and he sought a theme which would serve similarly his native Austria. The result was the famous *Gott erhalten unser Kaiser*, which was used in his "Emperor" quartet. To the words *"Deutschland über alles"* (*über* meaning not *over* but *above*, that is to say *in preference to*), the air provided the German national anthem. Eamonn Ceannt, perhaps by way of indicating that the enemies of England were Ireland's friends, wrote verses which scan to this tune. But he had not Kearney's gift for one thing, and, for another, the air, despite its perfectly concise and logical dignity, is foreign to Irish tradition, and moreover requires a language well supplied with feminine endings. The result is somewhat contrived.

IRELAND OVER ALL

Ireland's land and Ireland's nation
Ireland's faith and hope and song,
Irishmen will yet redeem them
From the foreign tyrant throng;
Ireland's home and Ireland's hillsides
Shall be freed from slavery;
Ireland, Ireland 'fore the wide world,
Ireland one and Ireland free!

Unity and right of freedom
For our Irish Fatherland,
Strive we all we may secure them,
Strive we all with heart and hand!
Be our aim then, God defending,
Right, eternal liberty!
Ireland, Ireland 'fore the wide world,
Ireland one and Ireland free!

One of the first organizations established as a result of renewed I.R.B. initiative was Na Fianna Eireann, (Soldiers of Ireland) a republican youth organization founded by Bulmer Hobson, the effective editor of *Irish Freedom*. When Hobson left Dublin for Belfast, Countess Markiewicz provided the premises and the inspiration. Na Fianna Eireann was the first organization of the period to undertake systematic training in the use of arms. When in the summer of 1913 members of the I.R.B. started drilling, they drew on the Fianna for instructors, as did also the Irish Volunteers founded at the end of the same year. The first full-time national organizer of the Fianna was Liam Mellows, who was made responsible for the Rising in south Galway. Six Fianna members fell as a result of Easter week, two of them, Con Colbert and Sean Heuston, being executed on 8th May, 1916. Barney Mellows, Liam's brother, and two other Fianna boys, Eamon Martin and Garry Holohan fought under Edward Daly in the Four Courts.

SONG OF FIANNA EIREANN

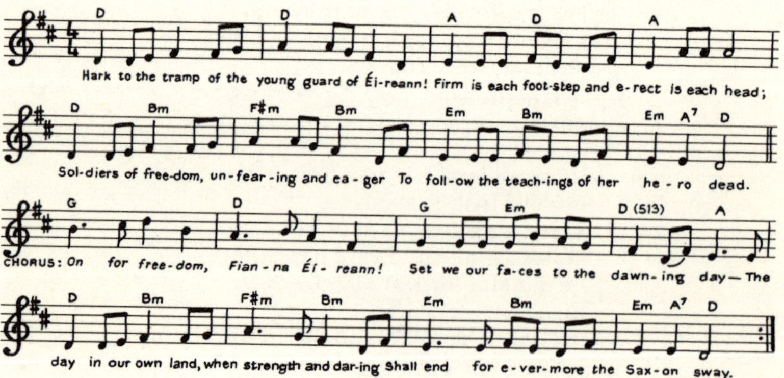

Strong be our hands, like the Fianna Eireann
Who won for her glory in the days that are gone;
Clean be our thinking and truthful our speaking,
That we may deserve her when the fight is done!

Chorus

Soldiers and champions of Eireann our Mother.
Fear we no Sassenach – his schemes or his steel,
Foes of the foeman, but comrades and brothers
Of all who are striving for our Eire's weal.

The Liberal Government was dependent for its majority on the Irish Parliamentary party whose policy was Home Rule, that is to say the delegation by Westminister of powers respecting purely Irish affairs to a subordinate legislature in Dublin. Since Gladstone's time Home Rule had been accepted Liberal policy also. But it was not until the Irish held the balance of power that the Liberals had to show the colour of their money. A Home Rule Bill was introduced in 1912. The Tory party responded by stirring up sectarian extremism in the north-eastern part of Ireland, where their favourite catchcry was that Home Rule would be Rome Rule. They went further; they made plans for establishing a Provisional Government and formed an extensive paramilitary organization, the Ulster Volunteers, who were prepared to defy Parliament if Home Rule were introduced. The organization went to the length of smuggling in arms from Germany, and their Tory leaders fomented a mutiny of officers stationed at the Curragh, when they were ordered to move north to protect Government military stores. It was the blatant preparation of armed counter-revolution that sparked off revolution. In November 1913 the Irish Volunteers were established in order to "secure and maintain the rights and liberties common to all the people of Ireland." This was the body which was later re-named Oglaigh na hEireann, the Army of Ireland, more usually known in English as the Irish Republican Army, or I.R.A. The formation of the Volunteers indicated a new degree of co-operation between the I.R.B. and the Parliamentarians who were now menaced by physical violence. The defence organization even enjoyed the support of British Liberals anxious for a counter-balance to Tory lawlessness. Within less than a year the Volunteers had recruited over a hundred thousand men, who were drilling throughout the country.

THE IRISH VOLUNTEERS

A hundred years of waiting,
Of sorrow and of pain,
And now the heart of Eireann
Beats high with hope again,

Chorus

Lift up the flag of Freedom,
And be your marching song
The music of the rifle –
'Tis clear and sweet and strong!

Chorus

Close ranks! too long they're broken,
Wipe out the wasted years;
March on, march on to Freedom
With Ireland's Volunteers.

Chorus

Brian O'Higgins

At an early stage a women's auxiliary organization was established. Many of its members came from the Women's Suffrage Movement which had deep historical roots in Ireland, going back to the novelist Maria Edgeworth. At the same time it is true that the place of women in Irish history has been profoundly affected by Ireland's status as a nation in permanent moral revolt. It would be a mistake to transfer judgments uncritically from English conditions to Irish. The subjection and degradation of women was Greco-Roman, not Celtic. If British schoolbooks do not make much of Boudicca, every Irish child knows about Granuaile, Grace O'Malley, the fighting clanswoman who stood up to Queen Elizabeth. The national struggle demanded the efforts of the women as well as the men. One thinks of Betsy Gray in 1798, of Anne Devlin, heroine of the insurrection of 1803 and of Constance Markiewicz, acting as second in command in St Stephens Green at the direct request of former soldier Michael Mallin.

Repeatedly in Irish history the women have carried the torch when the men were forced to relinquish it. When the leaders of the Land League were arrested, the Ladies Land League took over and kept the country in an uproar. In 1916 all the archives and secrets of the I.R.B. were passed to Mrs Tom Clarke, who, on the death of the former leader, took personal charge and had the I.R.B. re-established in less than a year. Thus while Irish women participated in the national movement within the framework of existing social conditions, there was also a powerful suffrage movement, through which two of James Connolly's secretaries, Winifred Carney and Mrs Tom Johnson found their way to socialism. Among the women wounded in action in 1916 was Margaret Skinnider. The women's auxiliary organization was known as Cumann na mBan.*

*When two letters of the same consonantal group stand together in this way, the first "eclipses" the second, and is alone sounded. Thus – approximately Cum'nn na Mawn.

THE SOLDIERS OF CUMANN NA mBAN

No great-hearted daughter of Ireland
Who died for her sake long ago,
Who stood in the gap of her danger,
Defying the Sassenach foe,
Was ever more gallant or worthy
Of glory in high sounding rann,
Than the comrades of Oglaigh na hEireann,
The soldiers of Cumann na mBan!

O, high beat the hearts of our Mother,
The day she had longed for is nigh,
When the sunlight of joy and of freedom
Shall glow in the eastern sky;
And none shall be honoured more proudly
That morning by chieftain and clan
Than the daughters who served her in danger,
The soldiers of Cumann na mBan!

Brian O'Higgins

For a number of years there had been no restriction on the importation of arms into Ireland. The Ulster Volunteers availed themselves to the full of this situation. But no sooner had the Irish Volunteers been established than a ban was clamped down. The English Government had no objection to drilling in Ireland. That might come in useful for the expected war with Germany. But possessing arms was another matter, especially for nationalists.

Early in August 1914, just before the war broke out, Erskine Childers brought into Howth a substantial cargo of arms procured in Germany, and these were landed with the aid of Na Fianna Eireann and distributed to the Volunteers. Of course the greater proportion of the guns used in 1916 were there before the Howth landing. But Childers's achievement stood as a kind of riposte to the much more substantial Unionist operation in Larne the preceding April. The possession of a Howth rifle became a matter of prestige. It might be worth noting in passing that Sean O'Casey's implication in his *Shadow of a Gunman* that there was ever a time when "there wasn't a gun in the country" provides an example of artistic rather than historical verisimilitude.

Robert Lynd was taken to task by P.S. O'Hegarty for suggesting that the origin of the Rising was to be sought in the great industrial struggle of 1913 rather than in the painstaking preparations of the I.R.B. Yet there are two senses in which Lynd was right. In August 1913 over four hundred employers banded together to refuse employment to members of the Irish Transport and General Workers' Union. The resulting lock-out lasted eight months and the result was a drawn battle. The men put their Union badges in their pockets and went back to work. After a few weeks they had them up again. In the course of these events the working class of Dublin for the first time realised its power. This was vital to the development of the revolution, the more so since the employers were openly identified with the Parliamentary party whom the I.R.B. regarded as its bitterest enemies. Second, in the course of the lock-out the employers used armed blacklegs and a workers' defence force, the Irish Citizen Army, was established a fortnight before the founding of the Volunteers, and became their ally in the struggle.

MY OLD HOWTH GUN

I was glad when you were near,
O, my old Howth Gun!
And no foeman did I fear,
O, my old Howth Gun!
For your bark and bitter bite
Put the Saxon curs to flight,
    And they wouldn't dare to fight
    O, my old Howth Gun!

How glorious was your feel,
O, my old Howth Gun!
When you made the Saxon reel,
O, my old Howth Gun!
When the Lancers trim and neat,
Charging down O'Connell Street,
    Had to beat a quick retreat,
    O, my old Howth Gun!

The parting it was sore,
O, my old Howth Gun!
Sure I ne'er may see you more,
O, my old Howth Gun
There was glorious hope that we
Could have set old Ireland free,
        Now you're parted far from me,
        O, my old Howth Gun.

But a day will come again,
O, my old Howth Gun!
When I'll join the fighting men,
O, my old Howth Gun!
With some brave determined band,
Proudly there I'll take my stand
        For the freedom of our land,
        O, my old Howth Gun!

Through this combination of circumstances the tradition of Irish socialism became an integral part of the Rising of 1916. There had been socialists in Dublin since the time of the First International and earlier, and it is of some interest that one of them, Jim Connell, who inclined to the Bakuninist wing in the struggle which ended the effective life of the International but who later emigrated to England and joined the Independent Labour Party, wrote the song which has always been especially associated with British Labour. It was not however intended to be sung to the tune "Tannenbaum", but to that of "The White Cockade", which is given here. The late Desmond Ryan used to tell a story of how Jim Connell attended a Labour conference in Britain in the early twenties and heard "The Red Flag" sung like a dirge. He followed the chairman after the conference was over and could do nothing but ejaculate over and over again, with deep reproach, "Ye sp'iled me pome! Ye sp'ild me pome." Here it is, unspoiled.

THE RED FLAG

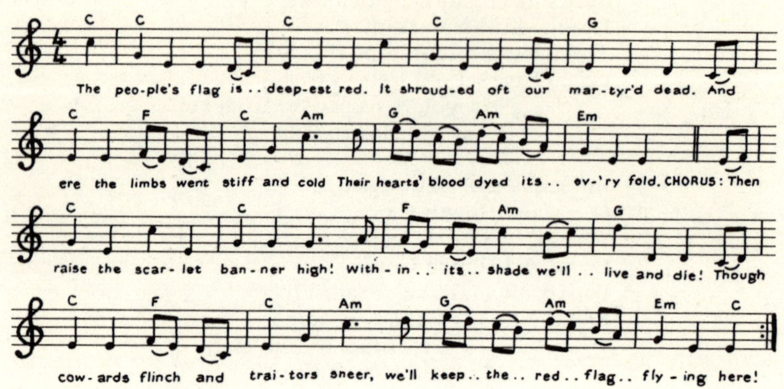

Look round! The Frenchman loves its blaze,
The sturdy German chants its praise,
In Moscow's vaults its hymns are sung,
Chicago swells the surging throng.

Chorus

It waved above our infant might
When all ahead seemed dark as night;
It witnessed many a deed and vow –
We must not change its colour now!

Chorus

It well recalls the triumphs past;
It gives the hope of peace at last;
The banner bright, the symbol plain
Of human right and human gain.

Chorus

It suits today the weak and base
Whose minds are fixed on pelf and place,
To cringe before the rich man's frown
And haul the sacred emblem down.

Chorus

With heads uncovered swear we all
To bear it onward till we fall,
Come dungeon dark or gallows grim,
This song shall be our parting hymn.

Chorus

Jim Connell

Connolly invited his hearers to join the Citizen Army at a public meeting on 13th November 1913. The port of Dublin had been closed "as tight as a drum" in protest against the continued imprisonment of the I.T.G.W.U. leader Jim Larkin. Larkin was released and set off to carry his "fiery cross" through England and call for sympathetic action. At the victory meeting Connolly began:

> I am going to talk sedition. The next time we are out for a march I want to be accompanied by four battalions of trained men with their corporals and sergeants. Why should we not drill and train men as they are doing in Ulster?

Captain White, ex-British officer and son of General Sir George White, undertook responsibility for training the new army. "Pawn your shirts to buy a rifle", urged the Countess Markiewicz somewhat optimistically since at that time not many of the workers possessed a shirt worth pawning. Soon the I.C.A. was drilling at Croydon Park, a large house with three acres of grounds that had been acquired as a recreational centre for members of the Union. After the conclusion of the lock-out, the I.C.A. continued as an independent armed force closely linked with the Union, but increasingly drawn into national politics. Notwithstanding its value in the lock-out, there were those in the Union who looked askance at it.

4th August 1914, was the day of the cataclysm, when the Pax Britannica dissolved in flames and ashes. Capitalism might still be an unconscionable time a-dying, but that day it received its death blow. Henceforth it was said George Russell had described the Dublin employers as "blind Samsons" pulling down the pillars on which their society rested. Now the two most powerful Empires on earth were smashing at those pillars on a world scale. Nothing like it had ever been known before. But the possibility had not been unforeseen. The Socialist International had resolved upon turning the expected imperialist war into a civil war against capitalism. Connolly decided that for Ireland this meant transforming it into a war of national liberation. On this matter, he and the I.R.B. were at one. An Irish Neutrality League was established and held a few meetings before, like the accompanying dissident press, it melted away in the heat of intensifying repression. A legal opposition was not to be tolerated.

The Irish Trades Union Congress, with which the Labour Party was combined, was one of the few national centres to declare against the war in the spirit of the resolutions of the International. The others were the Americans, the Russians and the Serbs. Apart from the Irish, the Labour movements of western Europe disgraced themselves. Larkin having gone to the United States in an effort to raise funds to meet the Union's staggering debts, Connolly raised over Liberty Hall the famous streamer, "We serve neither King nor Kaiser but Ireland." But it was made clear that Ireland had only one enemy.

The formal alliance between the Citizen Army and the Volunteers was sealed in January 1916. The I.R.B. had decided on an insurrection at Easter. Unaware of this Connolly was every week intensifying the propaganda of revolution in the *Workers' Republic*. Fearing that he would alert the authorities, the I.R.B. decided to take him into their confidence, and he made the seventh man on the military committee that was planning the Rising.

The I.R.B. had taken its decisions without informing the titular head of the Volunteers, Professor MacNeill, or their secretary Bulmer Hobson, though he indeed was one of their own members. The plan adopted was to announce manoeuvres, over which MacNeill would not need to be consulted, and to convert these into the real thing. Connolly was uneasy about attempting to "bounce" the Volunteers into insurrection, and indeed it was upon this weakness that the scheme foundered. When Hobson and MacNeill discovered that orders had gone out to turn the mobilization into an insurrection, they tried to have them countermanded. The result was that some units obeyed the one instruction, others the other. There was a reduced muster in Dublin, and in many areas no action was taken at all. And the Rising which was to have taken place on Easter Sunday took place on the Monday.

3

THE FIGHTING

> I desire now, lest I may not have an opportunity later, to pay homage to the gallantry of the soldiers of Irish freedom who have during the past few days been writing with fire and steel the most glorious chapter in the later history of Ireland. Justice can never be done to their heroism, to their discipline, to their gay and unconquerable spirit in the midst of peril and death. Let me, who have led them into this, speak in my own name, and in my fellow-commandants' names, and in the name of Ireland, present and to come, their praise, and ask those who come after them to remember them. For four days they have fought and toiled almost without cessation, almost without sleep, and in the intervals of fighting they have sung songs of the freedom of Ireland. No man has complained, no woman has asked "why?" Each individual has spent himself, happy to pour out his strength for Ireland and for freedom. If they do not win this fight, they will at least deserve to win it. But win it they will, although they may win it in death. Already they have done a great thing. They have redeemed Dublin and made her name splendid among the names of Cities.
>
> P.H. Pearse

Just what was the military plan of 1916? We know what happened. We do not know what was intended. Plans for a Rising were of course a commonplace of I.R.B. tradition, and from the outbreak of war, the subject must have been constantly under consideration.

There seem to have been two distinct components in the rebel strategy. The first was a general rising linked with the intended landing of German Arms at Limerick or Fenit. The provision of these arms was entrusted to Roger Casement whose arrival in Kerry synchronised with that of the arms ship and led to his arrest. They were to have been distributed by rail eastwards into Co. Cork, and northwards as far as Athenry. The object seems to have been to immobilize British forces in the interior while the second and principal effort took place in Dublin. A schematic plan for a rising in Dublin was drawn up by Joseph Plunkett. It was not dependent on the arrival of arms from abroad.

AN DORD FEINNE

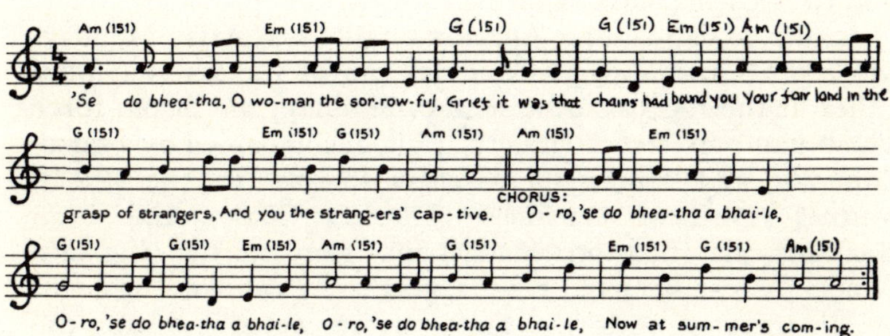

Granuaille comes over the ocean,
Men with arms as a guard about her,
Irish they, neither French nor Spaniard,
They will free her from the stranger.

Chorus

Thanks be to God if I should see it
Though I live but a week thereafter,
Granuaille and a thousand heroes,
Crying the rout of the stranger.

Chorus

The I.R.B. were dispersed throughout the Volunteers like steel in concrete. These could not move without the I.R.B. But the I.R.B. could not move them as they wished. The plan was to convert manoeuvres that were agreed into an insurrection which was not. There were conflicting loyalties. Already the bare fact of Casement's arrest was known in Dublin, and it was clear that little could be expected in the provinces. The result was that Plunkett's plan, though substantially adhered to, was deprived of its offensive significance. "We are going out to be slaughtered" said Connolly to William O'Brien as he left Liberty Hall. This was not a death wish, or a craving for martydom. It was a recognition that his forces were inadequate and it was too late to turn back.

Under a thousand men answered the call in Dublin, though the number grew to about sixteen hundred when it was seen that the fighting had begun.*

At the stroke of the Angelus on Bank Holiday Monday, while the Castle officials and leaders of the garrison were either at the races or otherwise on holiday, the mixed force which had mustered at Liberty Hall, accompanied by Pearse, Connolly and Plunkett, marched sharply to the G.P.O. whither the two civilians, Thomas Clarke and Sean MacDiarmada, had preceded them. They hustled the customers out, and started sandbagging the windows. The guard on the upper storeys was rapidly overpowered and soon the tricolour broke on the roof. Pearse, Connolly and Clarke stepped forward on the low plinth, and Pearse read the proclamation of the Irish Republic.

*A useful military assessment and map are to be found in *The Making of 1916 (Studies in the History of the Rising*, edited by Kevin B.Nolan) Stationery Office, Dublin, 1969.

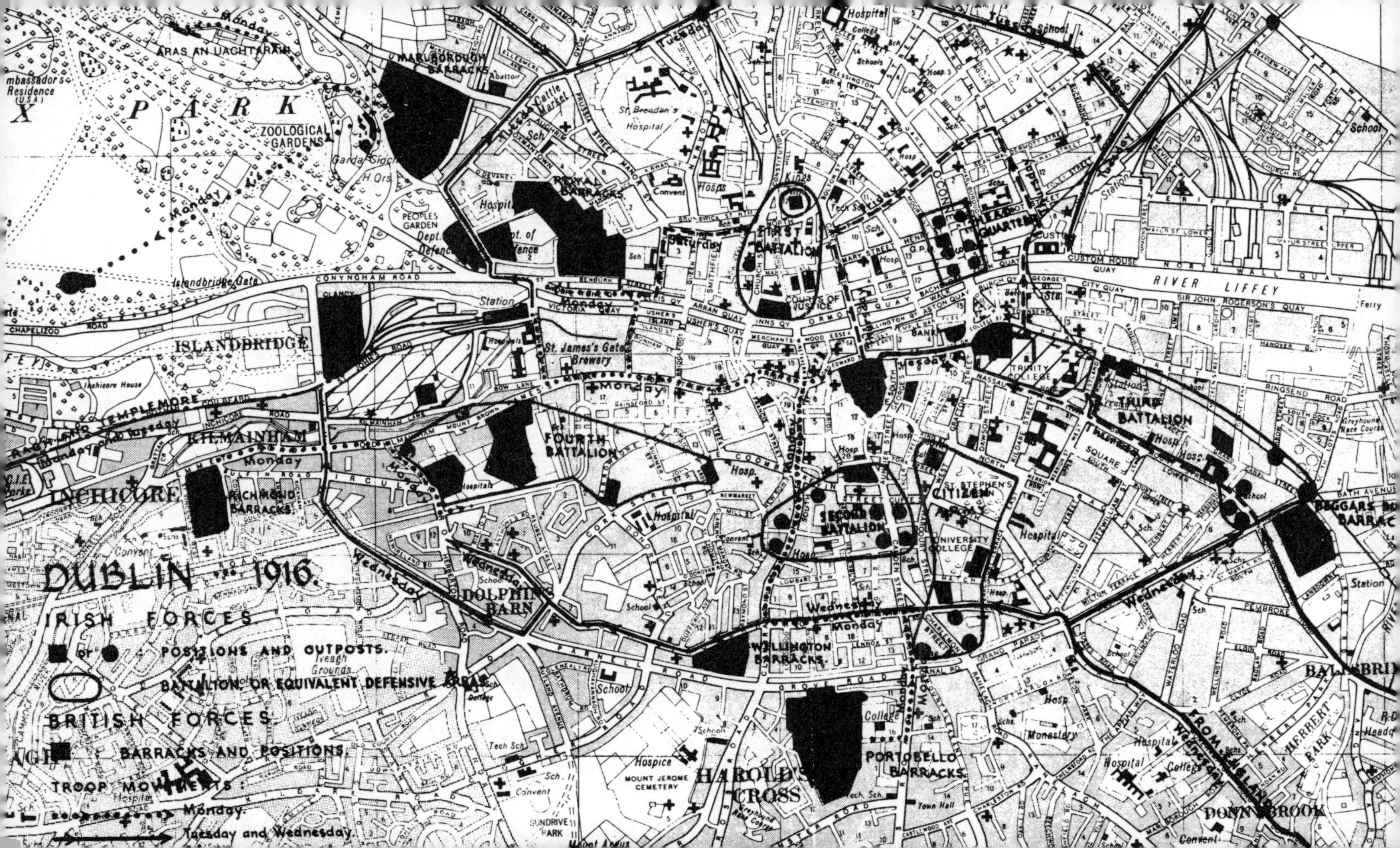
DUBLIN 1916
IRISH FORCES
or POSITIONS AND OUTPOSTS.
BATTALION OR EQUIVALENT DEFENSIVE AREAS
BRITISH FORCES
BARRACKS AND POSITIONS.
TROOP MOVEMENTS
Monday.
Tuesday and Wednesday.
FIRST BATTALION
SECOND BATTALION
THIRD BATTALION
FOURTH BATTALION
CITIZEN ARMY
HEADQUARTERS
MARLBOROUGH BARRACKS
ROYAL BARRACKS
RICHMOND BARRACKS
WELLINGTON BARRACKS
PORTOBELLO BARRACKS
BEGGARS BUSH BARRACKS
RIVER LIFFEY
PARK
ZOOLOGICAL GARDENS
ISLANDBRIDGE
KILMAINHAM
INCHICORE
DOLPHIN'S BARN
HAROLD'S CROSS
DONNYBROOK
TRINITY COLLEGE
UNIVERSITY COLLEGE
ST. STEPHEN'S GREEN
COURTS OF JUSTICE
St. James's Gate Brewery
FROM ENGLAND
Wednesday

Problacht na hEireann

The Provisional Government of the IRISH REPUBLIC To the People of Ireland

Irishmen and Irishwomen: In the name of God and of the dead generations from which she receives her old tradition of nationhood, Ireland, through us, summons her children to her flag and strikes for her freedom.

Having organised and trained her manhood through the secret revolutionary organization, the Irish Republican Brotherhood, and through her open military organizations, the Irish Volunteers and the Irish Citizen Army, having patiently perfected her discipline, having resolutely waited for the right moment to reveal itself, she now seizes that moment and, supported by her exiled children in America and by gallant allies in Europe, but relying first on her own strength, she strikes in full confidence of victory.

We declare the right of the people of Ireland to the ownership of Ireland and the unfettered control of Irish destinies to be sovereign and indefeasible. The long usurpation of that right by a foreign people and government has not extinguished the right, nor can it ever be extinguished except by the destruction of the Irish people. In every generation the Irish people have asserted their right to national freedom and sovereignty; six times during the past three hundred years they have asserted it in arms. Standing on that fundamental right and again asserting it in arms in the face of the world, we hereby proclaim the Irish Republic as a Sovereign Independent State and we pledge our lives and the lives of our comrades, to the cause of its freedom, of its welfare, and of its exaltation among the nations.

The Irish Republic is entitled to and hereby claims the allegiance of every Irishman and Irishwoman. The Republic guarantees religious and civil liberty, equal rights and equal opportunities to all its citizens, and declares its resolve to pursue the happiness and prosperity of the whole nation and of all its parts, cherishing all the children of the nation equally, and oblivious of the differences carefully fostered by an alien government, which have divided a minority from the majority in the past.

Until our arms have brought the opportune moment for the establishment of a permanent National Government, representative of the whole people of Ireland, and elected by the suffrages of all her men and women, the Provisional Government hereby constituted, will administer the civil and military affairs of the Republic in trust for the people.

We place the cause of the Irish Republic under the protection of the Most High God Whose blessing we invoke upon our arms, and we pray that no one who serves that cause will dishonour it by cowardice, inhumanity or rapine. In this supreme hour the Irish nation must, by its valour and discipline and by the readiness of its children to sacrifice themselves for the common good, prove itself worthy of the august destiny to which it is called.

Signed on behalf of the Provisional Government
Thomas J. Clarke
Sean MacDiarmada, Thomas MacDonagh,
P.H. Pearse, Eamonn Ceannt,
James Connolly, Joseph Plunkett

A glance at the map (page 57) will show that the insurgents had drawn a cordon round Dublin Castle. If the Castle could be taken, it could stand as their headquarters in the centre of their positions, with enormous psychological impact. The cordon would become its outer defence line. The Castle was attacked but it was not taken, and the reasons are obscure. One explanation is the death in action of Sean Connolly. Another is that the attack was not pressed as it was felt that the insurgents had insufficient men to hold it. The seizure of the Castle must have formed part of any plan for a rising in Dublin. But the confusion and postponement had reduced the insurgents' numbers. Once the Castle was not taken, the revolution was on the defensive. Headquarters remained at the G.P.O. which was completely exposed to

RALLY ROUND THE BANNER BOYS

What care we for the tyrant's power!
Our hearts are staunch and true.
Be ours the task to show once more
What Irishmen can do.
Let coward and hireling stand aside,
To linger still as slaves,
While we march on to freedom's goal,
Where Ireland's banner waves.

Then forward, men! On, on again!
Stout ships are on the sea,
And let us show the ancient foe
That Ireland must be free!
And while our banner floats on high,
Let every true man swear
To give his life in freedom's strife
To keep it floating there.

Come creed and clan, come every man;
We stand for Ireland all;
If from her chains she'll soon be free,
What matter if we fall?
Our flag unrolled – green, white and gold-
Inspired with hope once more,
While we march on to meet the dawn,
For slavery's night is o'er!

the north-east. This underlying strategic fact determined the course of the ensuing struggle. This is not to say, of course, that there was any plan to make Dublin Castle the headquarters, and that this was abandoned. It is to illustrate how seriously the insurgents' options were limited as a result of inadequate forces.

The English Government had 2,500 troops available for action on Easter Monday. They belonged almost entirely to Irish regiments. But they did not revolt. A dilemma argued over since the days of John Mitchel had reappeared. If a rising is prepared openly, its concluding preparations are liable to take place in jail. If it is prepared secretly nobody knows what it is for, or whether it is necessary. The answer to this conundrum is of course that insurrections demand more than preparations, they depend on opportunities, on political, social and military conditions being favourable. And they have to be very favourable to counterbalance the natural advantage of Government.

The Government tactics were first to remove the threat to the Castle and the English military barracks in the city; second to bring in reinforcements so as to immobilize the insurgents in their positions; and third to invest the Post Office and attack it on its unprotected north-eastern flank The first reinforcements, 1,600 in number, were brought from the Curragh on Monday afternoon, a further thousand being called for in the evening. Artillery was brought from Athlone, and more troops from Belfast.

On Tuesday four battalions of the Sherwood Foresters were moved from Watford to Liverpool whence they embarked for Dun Laoghaire in ships belonging to the Isle of Man Steamship Company. The English forces built up during the week had reached 12,000 when General Maxwell arrived in person early on Friday morning.

The rebel positions in the City Hall and the other buildings around the Castle had fallen by 3.00 p.m. on Tuesday afternoon, in spite of Connolly's efforts to reinforce them. That morning Mallin had been forced to retire from the Shelbourne Hotel to the College of Surgeons. He continued to hold down Crown forces, but apart from restricting the free passage of reinforcements, his garrison was thereafter of little effect. On Tuesday also, the English set up a line of posts from Kingsbridge station to Trinity College (something that might have been difficult if the insurgents had seized the Bank of Ireland) and began their investment of the Post Office from the north-east. They concentrated on main tasks and attacked rebel positions only when impeded by them. Thus the Mendicity Institution was attacked on Wednesday morning. Presumably it presented a threat to troop movements from Kingsbridge.

Perhaps the most spectacular resistance was that of De Valera's third battalion in the Bolands' Mill area. The Sherwood Foresters, advancing from Dun Laoghaire on Wednesday morning came under fire about half a mile from Mount Street bridge. Many of the Foresters were raw recruits with no more than six weeks' training. They had certainly no training in street fighting. And they did not know Dublin. Nevertheless the defence of this area by the rebels was a remarkable achievement. Their numbers were only seventeen. But when shortly before midnight the Crown forces finally cleared the way to the centre of the city, they had lost 230 men and decided not to proceed till morning.

In preparation for the attack on the Post Office, artillery was brought up to pound the buildings of central Dublin. On Wednesday Liberty Hall was shelled from Tara Street, although the Crown forces could hardly believe that it was occupied by insurgents. It had rebelly associations however, and it was probably thought a good plan to knock it down. The Royal Navy yacht *Helga* sailed up the Liffey and added her meed of destruction.

After the artillery barrage came the attack on buildings surrounding the Post Office which were occupied and searched while the investment proceeded on the north-eastern side. Gradually the English gained control of the streets, while the rebels developed a new defensive technique of burrowing through the walls from building to building. On Thursday morning Pearse admitted that the G.P.O. was isolated. The slow process of encirclement and compression continued throughout the day. Machine guns were posted on the roofs of buildings overlooking the insurgent headquarters. Artillery was brought into action again. It was on Thursday, while directing the setting up of the barricades intended to counter these movements, that Connolly was wounded severely in the leg. He continued to direct operations from a stretcher, but he was in acute pain, and there is good evidence that his powers of concentration were for a time impaired. Building after building went up in smoke and flames. By Friday morning the insurgent positions consisted of the Post Office, a few buildings behind it and the Metropole.

Early on Friday morning General Maxwell arrived to take charge of operations. He had had experience in Egypt. He confirmed the existing plan of operations. The sound of artillery grew more deafening all day. Machine guns rattled. Snipers were firing from every roof top not engulfed in flames. But the English did not take the Post Office. Its roof became untenable in the hail of fire. There was no means of extinguishing the incendiary shells which fell on it in ever increasing numbers. One of these set fire to the upper storeys of the building. Shortly after 8.00 p.m. after the wounded and the greater part of the women had been evacuated, Pearse, Connolly and four hundred of their followers made an effort to break out of their encirclement in a northwesterly direction.

They breached their own barricade, and despite heavy fire in which The O'Rahilly*lost his life, made their way into houses in Moore Street, tunnelling through walls in the hope of reaching Parnell Street where they might take up new positions. This called for immense courage, for the men had run singly across Henry Street under fire. Failing in their objective of reaching the Williams and Woods factory they had hoped to occupy, Pearse and Connolly realized that there was nothing further to be gained by persistence than avoidable slaughter. Miss Elizabeth O'Farrell was sent out under flag of truce at 12.45 p.m. on Saturday. Pearse surrendered to General Lowe at about 3.00 p.m. Though the other

*The definite article appertains to the chief of a clan.

THE DAY

Not in vain you poured your life-blood,
Gallant hearts of ninety-eight;
Not in vain you stood undaunted
'Neath the scourge of English hate.
Men of Wexford, men of Antrim
Men whose names shall ne'er decay
But still shine like stars to lead us
To the dawning of the day.

Chorus

Foreign foe and native traitor
Both have failed to quench the flame
That has guided Ireland's armies
Through the years of pride and shame.
And 'twill flush to deathless glowing
Making bright the upward way
When our men shall march to freedom
And the dawning of the day.

Chorus

O'er the fields your blood has hallowed
O ye hosts of Irish dead
In the light of freedom's morning
Men of Ireland yet shall tread.
When the foemen reel before you
In the thunder of the fray
They shall shout your name in triumph
At the dawning of the day

garrisons did not surrender till next day, the Rising was over.

Michael O'Rahilly who died in the last hours of the conflict was a remarkable man. He came from a well-to-do Kerry family and before finally establishing himself in Dublin in 1909, he lived in England and the United States. He became an adherent of Griffith's party, but joined the Volunteers at their inception. He was not a member of the I.R.B. but was considerably in their confidence. There is evidence that he played an important part in their reconciliation with Connolly in January 1916. He worked vigorously with Hobson and MacNeill to prevent a rising which he thought doomed to failure, but once the die was cast, presented himself at Liberty Hall with a motorcar for the transport of ammunition. He left a song, based on an earlier one which may serve as his epitaph (page 66-67).

Outside Dublin the most important struggle was in Galway. One of its participants remarked years afterwards that if the Rising in Dublin was dedicated to Thomas Davis, that in Galway was directed by the shade of Fintan Lalor, the great apostle of "the land for the people". Athenry, the important railway junction which was to be the final destination of the German arms, had for years been a hotbed of land agitation, which had spread to the town tenants. Something over 600 Volunteers came out and remained encamped at Moyode until news was brought that the fighting in Dublin had ceased. Though it may have been a Lalor rising, Davis's song was sung beside the camp fire (and how could it not?) in an atmosphere tense with optimism and excitement. Liam Mellows, the twenty-three-year-old leader, and his lieutenants, Frank Hynes and Alf Monaghan escaped to safety over the mountains when it was decided to disband.

THOU ART NOT CONQUERED YET DEAR LAND

Though knaves may scheme and slaves may crawl
To win their master's smile,
And though thy best and bravest fall,
Undone by Saxon guile;
Yet some there be, still true to thee,
Who never shall forget
That though in chains and slavery
Thou arc not conquered yet!

Chorus

Through ages long of war and strife,
Of rapine and of woe,
We fought the bitter fight of life
Against the Saxon foe;
Our fairest hopes to burst thy chains
Have died in vain regret,
But still the glorious truth remains -
Thou art not conquered yet!

Chorus

The O'Rahilly

THE WEST'S ASLEEP

That chainless wave and lovely land
Freedom and nationhood demand;
Be sure the great God never planned
For slumb'ring slaves a home so grand.
And long a brave and haughty race
Honoured and sentinelled the place.
Sing, Oh! not even their son's disgrace
Can quite destroy their glory's trace.

For often, in O'Connor's van,
To triumph dashed each Connacht clan,
And fleet as deer the Normans ran
Thro' Corlieu's Pass and Ardrahan;
And later times saw deeds as brave,
And glory guards Clanricarde's grave,
Sing, Oh! they died their land to save
At Aughrim's slopes and Shannon's wave.

And if, when all a vigil keep,
The West's asleep! the West's asleep!
Alas! and well may Erin weep
That Connacht lies in slumber deep.
But, hark! a voice like thunder spake,
The West's awake! the West's awake!
Sing Oh! hurrah! let England quake,
We'll watch till death for Erin's sake!

Thomas Davis

The only other considerable rising, that in north Co. Wexford, was also strongly influenced by Mellows, who had spent much of his childhood in the district. It was led by his friend Sean Etchingham, a journalist on the staff of the Enniscorthy Echo. About 600 Volunteers seized the town of Enniscorthy on the Thursday and parties entered the towns of Gorey and Ferns. They remained in the field until after the Dublin surrender. Etchingham was deported to England and imprisoned, and while in jail entertained his comrades with characteristic comic verses. The following, which has been supplied by the kindness of Miss Comerford, is said to have been composed on the train on the way to jail. It scans to Rooney's "Men of the West".

COWLD TAY

We watched out if anyone knew us,
    But got no reward for our pains,
As we journeyed from Dartmoor to Lewes
    Secured in our handcuffs and chains.
But soon other thoughts we were thinking,
    For 'ere we had reached the half way,
Like boys out of school we were drinking
    A glass of the cowldest of tay.

Chorus

So let us to England be grateful
    And trust her by night and by day,
And swear that 'rebellion' is hateful
    As long as she gives us cowld tay.

For she's out to save little nations,
Isn't that what her leading men said?
To prove it she's now on half rations
And fairly well stranded for bread.
So we rebels are resting contented,
Our feelings light hearted and gay,
For we see that "John Bull" is demented
And we toast his defeat in cowld tay.

Sean Etchingham
(13th December 1916)

There were small mobilizations in the Counties of Monaghan and Louth. Members of the R.I.C. were arrested at Castle Bellingham. Some of the Co. Louth men reached Dublin and fought in the Post Office. Some of the Belfast Volunteers mobilized at Coalisland in Co. Tyrone. There had been some notion of sending them to Galway, one suspects to spare them possible reprisals in the northern capital. In both the city and the County of Cork the great distance from Dublin made it virtually impossible to clear up the confusion of orders and the Volunteers reported for duty only to go home again.

But on Friday, the day before the surrender, there took place in north Co. Dublin the sole successful battle of the campaign. Thomas Ashe, with less than fifty men, all on bicycles, captured four police barracks and seized substantial quantities of arms and ammunition. The operation was of the guerrilla type which became standard practice four years later. Ashe was captured and imprisoned at Lewes. He died on hunger strike in Mountjoy prison in 1917.

No account of the Rising of 1916 would be complete without reference to Casement's gallant effort in Co. Kerry. By far the most distinguished participant in the insurrection, he paid the severest penalty. Not only was he imprisoned under extremely harsh circumstances, subjected to the indignities of long drawn out proceedings, and hanged as many believe, illegally; the massive demand for his reprieve was blunted, diverted and circumvented by the publication of judicious extracts from alleged diaries which purported to show him as a moral degenerate. The extracts were then withdrawn by the Government and have never been identified to this day. By the same token his fellow participants in vice and immorality have all vanished into thin air. He was hanged on allegations he was not given an opportunity to rebut. If their accusations had something in them, then the Government's action was still contemptible; if there was nothing in them, as many believe, then it was monstrous.

Casement was born in Co. Dublin in 1864. Following an appointment with a shipping line he travelled in Africa and took part in Sandford's expedition of exploration in the Congo. His lectures in the U.S.A. established his reputation as an expert on Central Africa.

After an appointment as travelling commissioner with the Niger Coast Protectorate, he became British Consul at Lourenco Marques, then Consul for Portuguese Africa with his residence at Luanda.

Having held a number of other consulages, he was selected to head an expedition sent to investigate allegations of gross atrocities committed against the natives of the Belgian Congo. He found a true bill against the rubber interests, and so impressive was his testimony that he was offered a knighthood but declined it.

After carrying out for the Foreign Office a further enquiry in the Amazon, and issuing another indictment of colonialist rapacity, he was knighted without being consulted and felt himself unable to withdraw. His family on his father's side had preserved the tradition of Protestant republicanism which informed the United Irishmen. He explained that his sympathy for the slaves of colonialism derived from his knowledge of the subjection of his own country. Feeling that in her fight for independence Ireland was entitled to accept help from England's enemies, he went to Germany soon after the outbreak of war. He negotiated with the Germans for an arms ship, and returned to Kerry by submarine, expecting to be met by Volunteers. He was captured among the sand dunes and brought to the Tower of London. A party of Volunteers had been sent to make the rendezvous. They took a wrong turning and their car plunged into Ballykissane harbour where they were drowned. From the time he was captured at Banna to the time of his execution his former colleagues showed Casement not the slightest mercy or consideration. This time he had exposed English imperialism.

LONELY BANNA STRAND

A motor car was dashing through the early morning gloom
A sudden crash and in the stream they went to meet their doom,
Two Irish lads lay dying there just like their hopes so grand,
They could not give the signal now from lonely Banna Strand.

'No signal answers from the shore' Sir Roger sadly said,
'No comrades here to welcome me, alas they must be dead,
But I must do my duty and at once I mean to land'
So in a boat he pulled ashore to lonely Banna Strand'.

The German ships were lying there with rifles in galore,
Up came a British ship and spoke 'No Germans reach the shore;
You are our Empire's enemy, and so we bid you stand
No German foot shall e'er pollute the lonely Banna Strand

They sailed for Queenstown Harbour. Said the Germans 'We're undone;
The British are our masters man for man and gun for gun,
We've twenty thousand rifles here, but they never will reach land
We'll sink them all and bid farewell to lonely Banna Strand.'

They took Sir Roger prisoner and sailed for London Town,
And in the Tower they laid him as a traitor to the Crown,
Said he, 'I am no traitor' but his trial he had to stand
For bringing German rifles to the lonely Banna Strand.

'Twas in an English prison that they laid him to his death
'I'm dying for my country' he said with his last breath;
He's buried in a prison yard far from his native land;
The wild waves sing his requiem on the lonely Banna Strand.

There can unfortunately be little doubt of the increasing brutality of the English soldiers, especially when they felt they were getting on top. Like many other revolutionaries in history the insurgents on their side could not at once put off the compunction of the civilian. They occupied houses but hesitated to use the family's furniture for barricades. The troops were not encouraged to cherish such prejudices. There was butchery and there was looting. Soldiers billeted on a Mr Beales paid him the compliment of drinking the tea he made for them before shooting him dead. There was little comfort for prisoners. At Richmond barracks they were placed in empty rooms without bedding or furniture. Sean MacDiarmada, who was lame, was deprived of his stick. All were subjected to the jeers of the soldiers as they were led away. The homes of suspects were searched and soon the deportations were in full swing as the leaders were shot in twos and threes, until somebody in the House of Commons said the executions were "becoming an atrocity."

4

THE AFTERMATH

The first executions, those of Thomas J. Clarke, Thomas MacDonagh and Padraig Pearse, took place on Wednesday, 3rd May. One of the great romantic heroes of Irish history, Pearse, though trained as a lawyer, devoted his life to two causes, the restoration of the Irish language and the establishment of a more humane system of education. He described English education in Ireland as the "murder machine". As a particular illustration of how Tory lawlessness begat revolution in Ireland, it is worth noting that until 1912 Pearse was in effect a supporter of the Parliamentarians. But by the end of 1913, he had thrown in his lot with the revolutionaries and joined the I.R.B. He and MacDiarmada became the driving force behind the war party in the organization. "The Dying Soldier" was written in memory of Pearse by Fr. MacThomas.

THE DYING SOLDIER

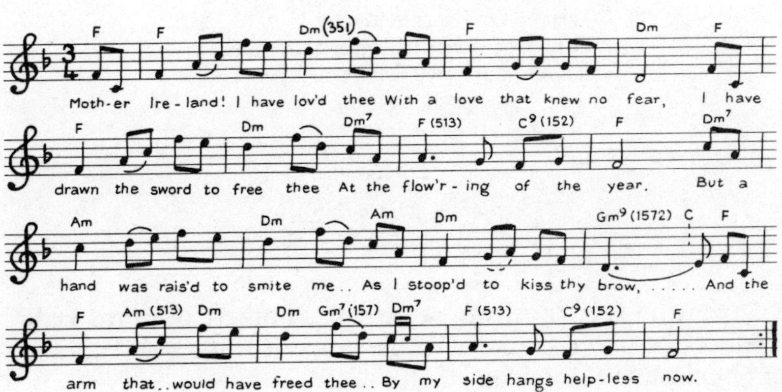

I have lived and loved and laboured
With a patriot's heart and will
That the dawning years might find thee
Fearless and unfettered still.
I am vanquished and my comrades
In the glorious fight have bled,
And the dauntless hearts that loved thee
Rest among the silent dead.

But 'twere nobler thus to perish
Thus to wipe away their tears,
With the distant voice of Freedom
Echoing in their dying ears,
Than to stand as fawning minions
Of the sneering conqueror's race,
With the clanking chains of bondage
Telling of our deep disgrace.

When the deathless glow of Freedom,
Flickering through the gloom of years
Shall have flashed upon the hilltops,
Conqueror of gloom and tears;
When a future age shall find thee
Freedom standing by thy side,
Mother Ireland, O remember
'Twas for Freedom's cause they died.

They are gone and I must follow
To the golden fields above,
Where the mighty God of Justice
Shall reward a patriot's love.
Sweet it were to live and love thee,
Sweeter far for thee to die,
With the flower-clad hills around me
Echoing back my last good-bye.

Next day it was the turn of Joseph Plunkett, Edward Daly (nephew of Tom Clarke), Willie Pearse (brother of Padraig) and Michael O'Hanrahan.

THE DEAD OF EASTER WEEK

No mother's hand upon their brow
No wife's fond kiss upon their cheek;
But in our hearts a silent vow,
The prayer our lips could scarcely speak.
'Tis good to think in gloomy days
When thoughts of dark despair arise,
Of these who walked the bloodstained ways
To meet their death with glowing eyes.

'Tis good to think that Ireland's call
Can gather still the leal and brave,
For her to give their lives, their all,
And win a soldier's lonely grave.
Some day a worthier song than mine
Their tale of noble deeds shall tell.
In Ireland's heart their names shall shine.
God rest them all - God rest them well.

On 5th May John MacBride was executed. He had taken no part in the preparation of the Rising, was in no sense a leader, but as a former member of the Irish Brigade that had fought on the side of the Boers in the South African war, he had joined the rebels once he saw the Rising started. He paid the supreme penalty thanks to the long memory and unassuageable malice of the English establishment. On the eighth there were four more executions, those of Con Colbert, Eamonn Ceannt, Michael Mallin and Sean Heuston. On the following day Thomas Kent was shot in Cork jail. His case falls somewhat outside the general pattern as he took no direct part in the rising.

The Kent family, consisting of an eighty-year-old woman and her four sons, lived at Bawnard House, Castlelyons, near Fermoy, Co. Cork. The family had been prominent in the Land League. They were leading Volunteers and the house was stuffed with every description of arms. Like Galway, Cork depended mainly on the arrival of the German arms. But it had no Mellows, whose escape from England (to which he was deported a few weeks before the Rising) and reappearance on the scene confirmed that the struggle was going to begin. The Volunteer leaders, Thomas MacCurtain and Terence MacSwiney were men of courage, integrity and high culture. But they were inexperienced. The succession of commands and countermands from Dublin, a hundred and sixty miles distant, fell into a sequence that was bound to cause total confusion. The intention had been to fight in the county. But the Kent family were still waiting for orders on the night of lst May, when a party of R.I.C. men surrounded the house and demanded its surrender. The Kents refused, and resisted all attempts to enter, resisted indeed with the old woman loading the guns and handing them to her sons, till the last bullet was expended. Head Constable Rowe was killed and several policemen were wounded. Richard Kent lost his life. His three brothers were arrested. Thomas Kent was court-martialled and executed on 9th May. If he had been a German he would have been made a prisoner of war. If he had been an Englishman he would have stood a civil trial. Being an Irishman he was taught law through the barrel of a gun.

By this time the protests had begun to mount. George Bernard Shaw had issued his courageous protest. "I remain an Irishman. And I am bound to contradict any implication that I can regard as a traitor any Irishman taken in a fight for Irish independence against the British Government, which was a fair fight in everything but the enormous odds my countrymen had to face." There were only two more executions, those of Sean MacDiarmada and James Connolly. Connolly, who had not recovered from his wounds and was not able to walk, was shot in a chair.

JAMES CONNOLLY THE IRISH REBEL

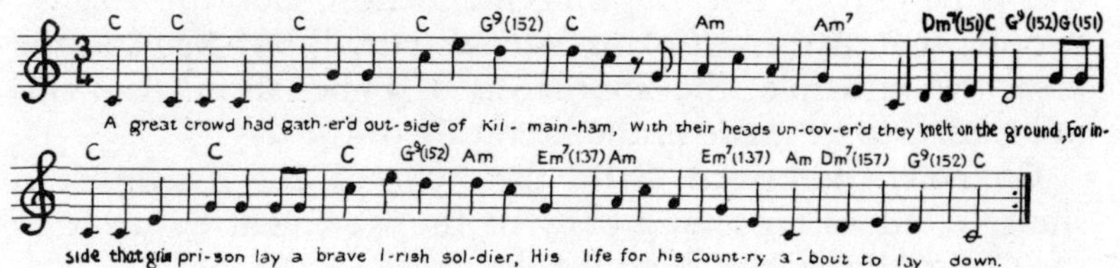

He went to his death like a true son of Ireland,
The firing party he bravely did face.
Then the order rang out: 'Present Arms, Fire,'
James Connolly fell into a ready-made grave.

The black flag they hoisted, the cruel deed was over,
Gone was the man who loved Ireland so well,
There was many a sad heart in Dublin that morning,
When they murdered James Connolly, the Irish Rebel.

God's curse on you, England, you cruel-hearted monster;
Your deeds they would shame all the devils in Hell.
There are no flowers blooming but the Shamrock is growing,
On the grave of James Connolly, the Irish Rebel.

Many years have rolled by since that Irish rebellion,
When the guns of Britannia they loudly did speak.
The bold I.R.A. they stood shoulder to shoulder,
And the blood from their bodies flowed down Sackville Street.

The Four Courts in Dublin the English bombarded,
The spirits of Freedom they tried hard to quell,
For above all the din rose the cry 'No Surrender,'
'Twas the voice of James Connolly, the Irish Rebel.

Perhaps it would be well to explain to English readers that the maledictions cast on England do not necessarily include themselves. It is not England the nation, nor the English people, that give rise to this intense hatred, but England the idea, the principle, the apotheosis of imperialism. And this point used to be made in the literature of the day.

Connolly contrived with the help of his daughter to smuggle out of hospital a copy of the statement he made to the Court Martial. He included the words:

> Believing that the British Government has no right in Ireland, never had right in Ireland, and never can have any right in Ireland, the presence in any one generation of Irishmen of even a respectable minority ready to die to affirm that truth, makes that Government forever an usurpation and a crime against human progress.

Sean MacDiarmada was born at Kiltyclogher in the Co. Leitrim. At the age of nineteen he emigrated to Glasgow where for a time he worked on the trams. He became interested in the work of the Gaelic League. Returning to Ireland he worked as a tram conductor and bar-tender. Through the Belfast Gaelic League he came into contact with Bulmer Hobson, and a while later he joined the I.R.B. He settled in Dublin in 1908 and became national organizer of the I.R.B., travelling the whole of Ireland on a bicycle. As a consequence of over-work he contracted poliomyelitis and was a virtual cripple for the last years of his life.

A SONG OF SEAN MacDERMOTT

For Connacht slumbered not, nor slept.
Adown her years of scourge and thorn,
But silently a vigil kept.
For some high resurrection morn;
And then it came; the very dust
Of storied hill and valley stirred,
When shroud and tomb aside were thrust,
And Easter flashed the gallant word.

Then Sean MacDermott fought his fight,
And paid the price that heroes pay,
Who with their brothers scale the height
Where men may face unfettered day;
Now Connacht bares her ancient head
Before the shrine, with eyes love-lit,
When on the roll-call of her dead
Brave Sean MacDermott's name is writ.

And not upon this shrine alone,
That name, sealed with his blood is set;
'Twill flame where noble deeds are done
In days unborn to history yet.
And men will feel their pulses thrill
To read of Erin's glorious scroll
Of those who broke a tyrant's will
And saved from him their country's soul.

Teresa Brayton

The last execution was that of Roger Casement, bringing the total to sixteen. Casement was hanged in Pentonville prison on 3rd August 1916. In Irish tradition he ranks below Connolly and Pearse who were at the centre of the maelstrom. But from the standpoint of the English ruling class he possessed a special importance. He had begun by exposing the crimes of other colonial powers. He had concluded by trying the English establishment as effectively as they tried him. The offer to accept a plea of "guilty but insane" based on the alleged diaries would have satisfied many people now in alliance with England, including the Belgian rubber barons. On the matter of the diaries, Mr Richard Deacon, historian of the English Secret Service, remarks that "the diaries bear all the signs of having been tampered with and of having salacious material inserted into them." He concludes that, "it was a nasty disreputable propaganda effort . . . totally unjustified even in the name of total war."

In addition to the sixteen sentences carried out, there were ninety-seven commuted to penal servitude, 160 courts martial and 122 sentences. Several thousand men and women were arrested without charge or trial and deported to prisons and internment camps in Britain. Official hysteria produced its invariable result, sympathy with the victims. In typically maladroit fashion, General Maxwell wrote to Dr O'Dwyer, Bishop of Limerick, urging him to silence priests who were believed to be expressing this sympathy.

The Bishop wrote to the General, "You took care that no plea for mercy should interpose on behalf of the poor young fellows who surrendered to you in Dublin. The first information that we got was the announcement that they had been shot in cold blood. Personally I regard your action with horror and I believe it has outraged the conscience of the nation."

BISHOP O'DWYER AND MAXWELL

Then answer made the brave O'Dwyer;
"My laws are not as thine,
For yours condemn in ruthless haste,
It is not so with mine,
Ere I'll accuse I'll know the charge,
The witness, place and time,
And ere I'll punish I'll have proof
That there had been a crime."

And quickly came the bogus charge,
In humble accents framed;
"Methought it needed naught to prove
The guilt of those I named.
They've hearkened to the rebels' word –
They've blessed the rebels' cause –
By voice and pen they've taught their flocks
To spurn the Empire's laws."

Our Bishop true no longer now
His anger can restrain;
His words are cutting as the scythe
That reaps the harvest grain;
"These men you name are Godly men,
In act and thought guilt free –
They serve their God and love their land,
And that's no crime to me."

"And were their guilt as black as night,
Don't think at your behest,
I'd join with those whose hands are dyed
In blood of Ireland's best.
Full many a ruthless English churl
Has held our land in thrall
But history sure will write you down
The blackest of them all.

"And do you think that I forget
My country's martyred dead;
The brave, the pure, the high-souled lads
Whose blood you foully shed?
Then here's your answer; I may share
The fate of those who died,
But I'll not be the first O'Dwyer
To take the tyrant's side".

Descendant of a noble clan,
May you be left us long –
Fearless and true to uphold our cause
'Gainst tyrants cruel and strong,
They thought that every voice was stilled,
That hearts were cold with fear;
No coward threats your heart could chill
Nor make your voice less clear.

And Oh! Thank God that there are men
To speak with love and pride
Of those who lie in prison cells
And those who nobly died.
And where the glorious tale is told,
Or Ireland's latest fight,
In letters golden shall be writ,
O'DWYER UPHELD THE RIGHT!

In the *Daily News* of 10th May 1916, George Bernard Shaw wrote:

> The shot Irishmen will now take their places beside Emmet and the Manchester Martyrs of Ireland, and beside the heroes of Poland and Serbia in Europe, and nothing in heaven or earth can prevent it.

During the next five years, whose positive outcome was the attainment of a measure of political independence for a part of Ireland that was subsequently materially enlarged, young people looked for inspiration to the men of 1916, as they in their day had looked to the Fenians. The heroism and sometimes almost naive magnanimity of the insurgents contrasts with the wizened cynicism of those who impelled the vast machine that was to suppress them, and the mean-spirited vengeance that was exacted.

It is tempting to speculate on what would have happened if it had been otherwise. If the ideal of an independent Ireland had not been anathematized by those in brief authority, if freedom had not been sidetracked by partition, would England have been worse off? Would her problems have been greater, her crisis more severe? Or might a few young people who died quite recently still be enjoying the sun? And if Irish separatism sometimes appears in dark and implacable colours, can we exonerate those whose unforgiving ferocity has left repeated scars on the folk-memory of an ancient people? The sigh of the lover and the gaiety of the Volunteer soldier mingle in the ballads of Easter week with an unyielding hatred of imperialism and a passionate determination that Ireland will yet be free.

THE THREE-COLOURED RIBBON

His bandolier around him, his bright bayonet shining,
His short service rifle, a beauty to see;
There was joy in his eyes though he left me behind him,
And started away for to set old Ireland free.

Chorus

He whispered Goodbye, love, old Ireland is calling.
High over Dublin our tricolour flew.
In the streets of the city the foeman is falling
And wee birds are saying "Old Ireland; arise!"

Chorus

In praying in watching the dark days passed over,
The roar of the guns brought no message to me.
I prayed for old Ireland, I prayed for my lover,
That he might be saved and old Ireland be free.

Chorus

The struggle was ended, they brought me the story,
The last whispered message he sent unto me.
"I was true to my land, love, I fought for her glory,
And gave up my life for to make Ireland free."

Chorus

THE DUBLIN BRIGADE

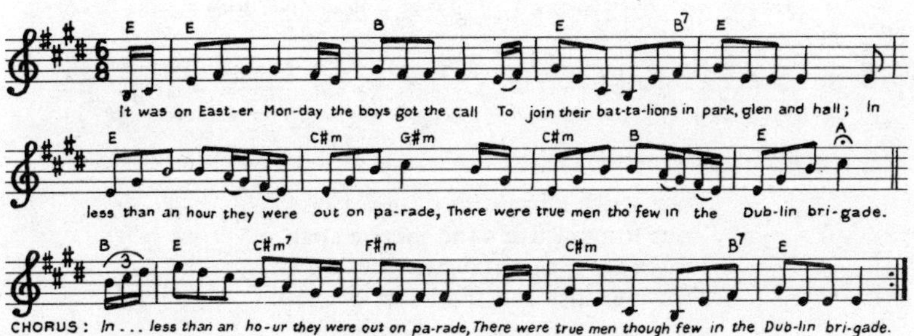

When they got their orders they took up their posts
Though few were their numbers 'gainst England's proud hosts;
There was joy in their hearts, not a man was afraid;
There were straight men and great in the Dublin brigade.

There was much work to do in getting things right
But the old and the young were all anxious to fight.
Every man worked hard at his own barricade,
And rifles rang out from the Dublin brigade.

They have shot down our leaders and sent us to jail;
They have broken the spirit, they think, of the Gael.
But the day will come yet when they'll all be afraid
Of the true fighting men of the Dublin brigade.

And now, goodbye – or, in Irish, slan libh.

SLAN LIBH

Your work allows no time for rest,
Your longest life's the merest span;
Your cause, the bravest, noblest, best,
That e'er inspired the heart of man.
Fight on! fear not! for God is just
(The tyrant too shall cease to live)
And pray for him whose bones are dust.

Chorus

Slan Libh! a simple Irish phrase
Of parting but to meet again,
Twixt comrades who thro' nights and days
For Eire's sake strove might and main;
For her dear sake, remember me.
For her dear sake my faults forgive.
God speed the fight for liberty!

Chorus

Lyric: Peader Kearney
Music: Sean Barlow

DUBLIN 1916
IRISH FORCES
POSITIONS AND OUTPOSTS.
BATTALION, OR EQUIVALENT DEFENSIVE AREAS
BRITISH FORCES
BARRACKS AND POSITIONS.
TROOP MOVEMENTS:
Monday.
Tuesday and Wednesday.
Thursday, Friday and Saturday.
ARTILLERY FROM ATHLONE
Tuesday
Monday
CURRAGH
Monday and Tuesday
TEMPLEMORE
Wednesday
CABRA
PARK
ZOOLOGICAL GARDENS
ARAS AN UACHTARAIN
MARLBOROUGH BARRACKS
ROYAL BARRACKS
ISLANDBRIDGE
KILMAINHAM
INCHICORE
RICHMOND BARRACKS
FOURTH BATTALION
DOLPHINS BARN
St. James's Gate Brewery
Cattle Market
Dominican Convent
Deaf & Dumb Institution
Apostolic Nunciature
Ambassador's Residence (USA)
St. Vincent's Home
Cabra Gate
Cabra Lodge
Islandbridge Gate
Conyngham Road
Chapelizod Road
Victoria Quay
Station
Peoples Garden
Dept. of Defence
St. Brendan Hospital
C.I.E. Works
Sundrive Park
Mount Argus
Mount Jerome Cemetery

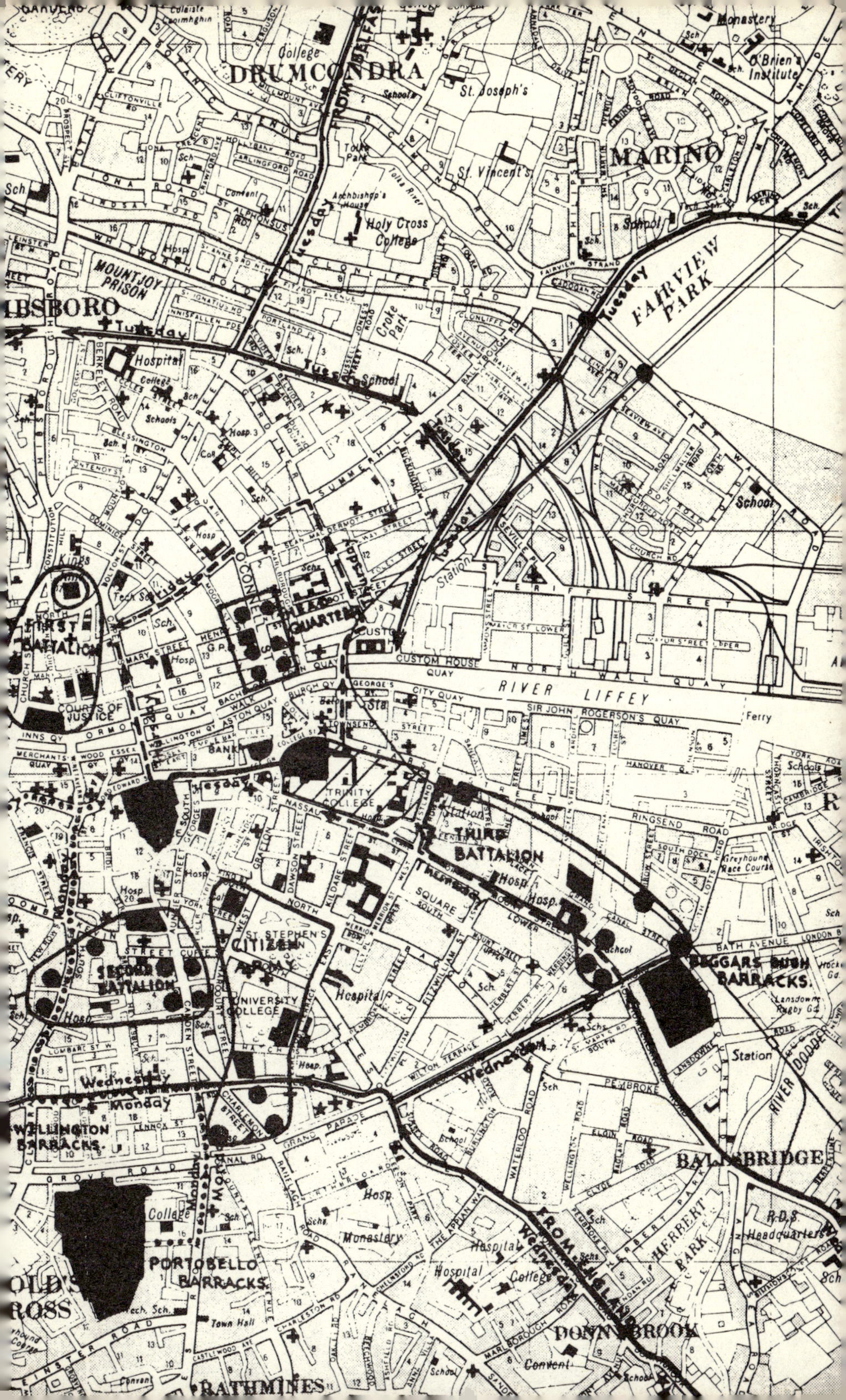
DRUMCONDRA
College
St. Joseph's
O'Brien's Institute
Monastery
MARINO
St. Vincent's
Tolka Park
Archbishop's House
Holy Cross College
School
MOUNTJOY PRISON
Croke Park
FAIRVIEW PARK
Tuesday
Hospital
School
Station
FIRST BATTALION
HEADQUARTERS
G.P.O.
CUSTOM HOUSE QUAY
NORTH WALL QUAY
RIVER LIFFEY
SIR JOHN ROGERSON'S QUAY
Ferry
COURTS OF JUSTICE
Bank
TRINITY COLLEGE
THIRD BATTALION
RINGSEND ROAD
Greyhound Race Course
BATH AVENUE
BEGGARS BUSH BARRACKS.
Lansdowne Rugby Gd.
ST. STEPHEN'S
CITIZEN ARMY
SECOND BATTALION
UNIVERSITY COLLEGE
Hospital
Wednesday
Monday
WELLINGTON BARRACKS.
GRAND PARADE
PEMBROKE
RIVER DODDER
BALLSBRIDGE
R.D.S Headquarters
HERBERT PARK
FROM ENGLAND
Monastery
College
PORTOBELLO BARRACKS
Town Hall
DONNYBROOK
Convent
RATHMINES